PIGS DO FLY!
MYSTERIES FROM THE BEYOND

ROBERT DUFFY

POOLBEG

Published 1998
by Poolbeg Press Ltd
123 Baldoyle Industrial Estate
Dublin 13, Ireland

© Robert Duffy 1998

The moral right of the author has been asserted.

A catalogue record for this book is available from the British Library.

ISBN 1 85371 843 2

Cover illustration by Leonard O'Grady
Cover design by Poolbeg Group Services Ltd
Set by Poolbeg Group Services Ltd in Stone 10/14
Printed by The Guernsey Press Ltd,
Vale, Guernsey, Channel Islands.

CONTENTS

INTRODUCTION

A neighbour of mine, Michael Connolly, is often called upon to help Gardaí locate missing persons. His most notable success was a tragic tale – a body was fished from the River Slaney along a section where he suggested that they look. Like all clairvoyants, however, Michael's record has its fair share of failure as well as success. His powers are normally called upon for a more everyday reason: he is a successful water diviner.

I have often spoken to Michael about his talent and I have shared with him many of the tales that make up these *Unexplained Mysteries*. Why does he have the gift and others don't? I once asked him. He believes that we all have it, that it is just a matter of sensitivity. There are forces all round us, acting on us all the time. Some of us feel them; most of us don't.

"Hold on a minute, Robert," Michael said before he strolled over to his car. He returned with two unsophisticated pieces of equipment: L-shaped pieces of wire cut from an old coat hanger. Michael preferred these tools to the conventional Y-shaped twig that we normally associate with water diviners. He taught me how to hold them, how to relax my grip and let the forces work on the flimsy wires.

Following his instructions, I walked along the street. I was astonished when the two parallel wires in my

1

hands crossed over. I had found water! As I walked along, the wires gently uncrossed as I moved away from the path of water flowing beneath the ground. Eventually, I came across a drain cover and I lifted the lid. Examining the flow of water within the drain, I confirmed that the two wire rods had led me along the route of its underground path.

Pigs Do Fly contains many fascinating case-studies and anecdotes. They come in many shapes and forms – Irishmen and Irishwomen who have delved into the unknown; evidence that ancient civilisations used technology that we thought came along in the twentieth century; and many, many more.

During my research, I came across the writings of eminent scientist and author Arthur C Clarke. He divides the paranormal and the unexplained into three simple subcategories:

Mysteries of the First Kind are ones that, from our ancestors' point of view, were completely awe-inspiring and unexplainable but are fully understood by us today. Imagine the wonder our forefathers must have felt as they watched red, orange, yellow, green, blue, indigo, and violet bands of colour sweep across a sundrenched sky? It was not until 1704 that Isaac Newton held his glass prism in a beam of light and demonstrated that white light as we know it is made up of the seven colours of the rainbow. A rainbow is still a beautiful, wondrous sight, but we know that it is caused by sunshine passing through crystal-clear drops of water in the sky.

Mysteries of the Second Kind are items that appear to be mysteries, but we know in our hearts that the explanation would be simple if only we had more information. Read about the Roswell Incident where locals claim that, in 1947, an alien spaceship crashed nearby. Roswell, in New Mexico, is close to a military base and the real answer to this riddle was probably hidden in the top secret files of the generals at the time. Within the next few decades the truth about the Roswell Incident – a Mystery of the Second Kind – might surface and the whole story might be no more mysterious than the rainbow question which Newton solved centuries ago.

Mysteries of the Third Kind are more frustrating. As yet we have no hope of solving them. Voices from the dead and the work of celebrated mediums could fall into this category except for the untiring efforts of magician Harry Houdini. Houdini really wanted to believe in spiritualism and he spent a large part of his life trying to find a genuine spiritualist medium. Invariably he found them to be tricksters with "magic" skills similar to his own. Arthur C Clarke gives his own example of a Mystery of the Third Kind. When a human body is cremated, searingly high temperatures have to be used and even then many of the bones remain intact, however, there are notable cases of spontaneous combustion where people have been reduced totally to ashes without surrounding furniture or clothes being damaged.

Dip in and out of *Pigs Do Fly: Unexplained Mysteries*. There's something here for everyone. Don't be a blind believer – or a cynical sceptic. Some of these accounts are presented as if they are true.

Just keep an open mind.

3

THE ISLAND OF THE PELICANS

Prisoners were beaten, stripped naked and tossed into cold concrete cells deep within the fortress on *La Isla de Los Altraces* – the Island of the Pelicans – better known as Alcatraz. Tourists now roam the horror corridors of this old fort which housed America's most dangerous criminals. Sightseers, their guides and several old prison guards have heard inexplicable sounds of screaming, running and the clanging of metal cups off the iron bars of the prison cells – sounds which, it is widely believed, belong to the ghosts of former inmates.

Banjo music drifts eerily from the showers. One hated inmate used to find peace there, playing his banjo, once a week when he was allowed to shower. Al Capone was that lone prison musician! Having pulled the strings of Chicago's underworld, he ended up a mad banjo player in the most notorious of America's federal prisons.

Ghosts roam most noisily in the infamous "Block D", the solitary confinement section where the authorities broke the spirit of rebellious prisoners. Rufe McCain was thrown into Cell 14-D and left to rot for over three years in the dark, damp, cold hole in the Rock. He had tried to escape with other inmates in 1939. The guards were watching, waiting for the prisoners after a tip-off. McCain was certain that one of his mates was the traitor. The mad, frenzied McCain slaughtered his comrade within hours of his release from "solitary".

Suicides, madness, murders and mutilations pepper the history of this rocky crag in San Francisco Bay. One crazed prisoner, fed up of his dreary routine and crying out for attention, horribly mutilated himself. He placed his hand on a bench in the prison workshop, swung an axe and chopped off his fingers.

Blood washed the walkways and spilled into the sea after an escape attempt went violently wrong in 1946. In desperation, prisoners with nothing to lose killed three guards. Other guards gunned down the would-be escapees, killing three of them. Several more were badly wounded. Clanging and moaning sounds are often heard along the corridor where the three 1946 prisoners lost their lives.

The infamous solitary cells of Block D, however, are the part of the prison where the most visitors have felt chills shivering up and down their spines. McCain's cell, 14-D, is always cold, regardless of how much the hot summer sun heats the infamous Rock of Alcatraz.

PIGS DO FLY

In August 1997 a whirlwind struck deep within the British midlands. It sucked forty pigs into the air and scattered them around the countryside. Unfortunately, this is not a story with a happy ending. The poor pigs – and their heavy pens – were hurled to the ground and the animals died. Locals were treated to the spectacle of pigs swirling 100 feet in the air – like a scene from the blockbuster film *Twister*.

{A cow survived a similar experience and lived to moo the tale. See the scroll after The Devil's Footprints file.}

Pigs do Fly! is littered with stories about things swirling through the sky or falling to earth. Here are some of the most bizarre stories:

Green Ice. A 10-kilo chunk of green ice landed on waste ground near a school in Tennessee in 1978. It roared to the ground and tossed up a small cloud of dusty earth. Such green ice incidents are dangerously commonplace in America and there is a logical explanation for them. Several Denver households have had green ice cubes smashing through their roof tiles. Or how about the Kentucky farmer who investigated the green ice that landed on his patch? He licked it several times, wondering if its taste would give any clue to its origins. He reported his find to the authorities and, to his horror, he found out what the green ice actually was – frozen waste from the toilet of a plane passing overhead!

Raining Blood. Red rain baffled our ancestors. Was it a sign of some great disaster about to happen – or was God warning us to mend our ways? When our cars and pavements are covered by red dust nowadays, we simply tune in to the weatherman and find out about wind patterns carrying dust from North African desert storms and dropping it on our shores.

Flying Meat. On a calm, cloudless day in Kentucky in 1876, a Mrs Crouch witnessed morsels of meat the size of snowflakes falling to earth. Some people gathered up this strange stuff and examined it. One gentleman said that the meat was venison (deer meat); another thought it was mutton (sheep). Scientists were called in to investigate the meat. They concluded that it was lung tissue – either from a horse or a human infant. The incident has never been explained. The theory at the time was that a flock of buzzards passing overhead had all felt a little airsick.

Raining Fish & Frogs. There are several reports of fish, frogs, eels or slugs falling from the air. A typical incident happened in France in 1794 when Napoleon's troops were fighting the Austrians near the village of Lalain, France. A sudden downpour caused 150 French soldiers to abandon their trench because the water was rising rapidly. The storm lasted for about thirty minutes and, in the middle of it, tiny frogs and tadpoles landed on the ground and slithered about the place. When the rains finally stopped, soldiers found the little creatures swimming in the brims of their hats. These incidents are usually explained by freak tornadoes sucking up water, carrying it and dropping it elsewhere. But why is it that these freak tornadoes are so selective – usually just picking up one species and ignoring all others?

Watch out for Mir! The Russian space station Mir is due to be abandoned in 1998. Once the computers and booster rockets are no longer keeping it on course, the station will drift into a shallower and shallower orbit and will eventually fall to earth like a meteorite. In 1962, a chunk of a Soviet sputnik satellite fell to earth in Wisconsin, USA. In 1979, America's space station Skylab fell into the Indian Ocean. The imminent arrival of the Skylab was well publicised. Its path in space took it over Ireland briefly. Opportunists in Australia and America took to the streets selling anti-Skylab helmets.

MESSAGE IN A BOTTLE – ONE

In 1952, New Zealander Ross Alexander ran aground on a reef off the coast of north-western Australia. While waiting to be rescued he scribbled out an SOS note and tossed it overboard in a wine bottle. Back home in New Zealand in 1955, the seaman went for a stroll along his local beach. There he saw a wine bottle bobbing in the water. He scooped it up, opened it, and discovered the message he had written three years earlier!

THE HAZARDS OF SHIPPING BARRELS OF ALCOHOL

Captain Briggs never took a drink. He plied his ships across the Atlantic and never allowed his crew to bring a drop of alcohol on board. He was a faithful family man, not interested in being unfaithful in ports thousands of miles from home. In fact, when he was detailed to ship a cargo from New York to Genoa in November 1872, he brought his wife and daughter with him. His son stayed behind in school in Massachusetts.

His cargo on this trip was to be something he hadn't handled before. Down in the hold he carried 30,000 dollars worth of alcohol. Would this be a problem with the crew that he insisted on keeping "dry"? Not really. The oak barrels contained undrinkable crude industrial alcohol.

On November 5 1872, the ship left New York and headed for Europe. To an experienced seaman like Briggs, the North Atlantic route was the equivalent of a well-worn trail: east-south-east from New York, sail south of the Azores and through the Straits of Gibraltar. Once in the Mediterranean head north-east for the Italian port of Genoa.

Industrial alcohol – or any alcohol – is explosive stuff. Heat it up and shake it about and it is going to expand. Wooden containers can creak and crack and flammable vapours can escape. Provided you know what you are handling, there shouldn't be a problem. Accept that some leakage is going to happen, keep away naked lights and heat from the alcohol and allow plenty of air to circulate.

But Captain Briggs had never carried industrial alcohol before. As he crossed the Atlantic, his ship was lightly tossed around by a normal share of ocean storms. Later in his voyage the weather became warmer. He was sailing from the icy conditions of New York through the warmer climate in the mid-Atlantic and beyond. His cargo expanded and gurgled, making the wooden barrels creak and leak. Being a good captain, Briggs probably had the hold well sealed to keep water out.

As the cargo warmed up, the air became heavy with the pungent vapour of alcohol. Air pressure within the hold increased, pushing against the snug-fitting hatch like an ox against a barn door. Suddenly, a harmless but frightening explosion was heard by the hands on deck. A nervous Captain Briggs and some crew members went down to investigate.

The hold reeked of alcohol. The liquid grumbled, gurgled and hissed in its barrels. An apron of the fluid sloshed about on the timber floor. Deeper within the hold the captain saw an ominous cloud of smoke oozing through the dim light.

"What is that stuff?" he might have said. "Quick! Open a barrel!"

Somebody wedged a crowbar into the lid of a barrel and pushed. Like a champagne cork – only louder – the lid blew, echoing around the confined space the men were standing in.

"Let's get out of here! Now! The whole lot is ready to explode. Move! Move!"

The captain's wife, Sarah, had finished her breakfast but hadn't made the beds yet. There was no time for that now. The ship might explode. They could be doomed. Hurriedly, the captain ordered their one lifeboat to be launched and all hands clambered aboard. The ship could go at any second and the only chance they had of surviving was in their little boat, tethered to the ship but floating a safe one hundred yards away.

While the crew scurried into the lifeboat, the captain had the presence of mind to dash back to the bridge and pick up his chronometer, sextant and navigation papers. If the ship blew and they had no way of working out a course in their little boat, they were doomed anyway. Briggs knew they were close to the Azores, close enough to sail to in the lifeboat. They could survive a couple of days without food. Having the navigation equipment meant they had a chance of surviving their ordeal, even if their ship was swallowed by an alcohol fireball.

They sat drifting in the midday sun, waiting for the fearful explosion and the destruction of their ship. Nothing happened. After their hasty departure fresh air circulated through the open hatches, defusing lethal vapours in the hold. As the sun sank into the western horizon the captain made the decision to board his ship again. They yanked at their towrope and pulled themselves back towards the ship.

Suddenly a gust swelled the waters beneath them, nothing serious to a sea-going ship but lethal for the flimsy little craft the crew were drifting in. The towrope yanked loose and a swollen wave engulfed them. Captain Briggs, his wife, his daughter and all his crew were drowned. No bodies were ever found.

The ship drifted lazily eastwards towards Europe. On 15 November, Captain Moorehouse, sailing on a ship named *Dei Gratia*, discovered the abandoned ship drifting halfway between the Azores and the coast of Portugal. The name of the abandoned ship? The *Marie Celeste*.

Because the *Marie Celeste* was found in such good condition and without any signs of a struggle, many bizarre theories were put forward about what happened.

10

Maybe a giant squid with long tentacles plucked out the crew one by one; maybe the crew was abducted by aliens. Contrary to reports at the time, the lifeboat was missing and there was not a meal cooking in the galley. There was also the theory that the crew of the *Dei Gratia* murdered their counterparts on the *Marie Celeste*. This possibility was thoroughly investigated and Moorehouse and his crew were found totally innocent of any wrongdoing.

No one will ever know exactly what happened on board the *Marie Celeste*, but the story outlined above is the most plausible and fits in with the known facts.

Although sailors gossiped amongst themselves about the mystery of the *Marie Celeste*, it was twelve years before the story entered the public domain. A young Scottish doctor heard about the ship and published a story about it twelve years after the abandoned vessel was discovered in the Atlantic. The *Cornhill Magazine* published the story in January 1884. The real name of the ship was the *Mary Celeste,* but the writer changed it to the more romantic-sounding *Marie Celeste* and the name stuck. The doctor-author was Arthur Conan-Doyle, who later shot to fame with his Sherlock Holmes stories.

THE ARCHDUKE'S CAR

As they were driven through Sarajevo in July 1914, the Archduke Franz Ferdinand and his wife were shot dead. He was heir to the throne of the Austro-Hungarian Empire and his death sparked off a chain of events that led to World War I. His car finally ended up in a museum in Vienna – but not before it was involved in a bizarre sequence of death and injury.

11

General Potiorek of the Austrian Army used the car and was jinxed by bad luck. After his defeat by Serbian forces the disgraced General died insane. While the car was not directly involved in that General's hard luck, one of his captains died at the wheel. In a road accident, the captain killed two peasants and was himself killed when the car swerved into a tree.

When World War I ended, the Archduke's car fell into the hands of the Governor of the newly-formed state of Yugoslavia. This unfortunate man suffered four non-fatal accidents with the vehicle, losing his arm in one of them. Later on the car became the property of a doctor. There were no witnesses to the event but, six months later, the hapless doctor was found crushed to death beneath the overturned car.

A jeweller committed suicide while he owned the Archduke's car, and a Swiss racing driver was killed when it struck a wall in the Italian Alps. A Serbian farmer was injured in a freak accident when, one day, he couldn't get the old car to start. He persuaded a passing farmer to give him a tow with his cart. The car chugged to life, smashed into the back of the cart and overturned on a bend.

The car was repaired yet again, this time by a garage owner. This mechanic, Tibor Hirschfeld, was the last person to own the jinxed car before it was taken to an Austrian museum. Returning from a wedding, Hirschfeld tried overtaking another car at high speed. He and four companions were killed. The ill-fated car, connected to the start of World War I and several fatal accidents, is still parked in that Vienna museum today.

12

COLUMBUS DID NOT DISCOVER AMERICA

A European child was born in America over 480 years before Christopher Columbus's famous voyage. In fact, at least a dozen different missionaries or adventurers may have reached the New World before Columbus set sail with the *Santa Maria*, the *Niña* and the *Pinta* in 1492.

Look at the story of our own St Brendan. In the 6th century AD, Brendan and other monks made pilgrimages across the sea in a rugged leather-hulled curragh – similar to the boats used by fishermen off Ireland's west coast today. For seven years Brendan's crew braved the cruel Atlantic and reached Iceland, Greenland and the North American coast around Newfoundland. Some accounts claim that Brendan then ventured southwards and reached the Caribbean. Two old manuscripts, *The Voyage of Saint Brendan the Abbot* and the *Book of Lismore,* confirm his travels in the North Atlantic. Tim Severin, a modern adventurer, has re-enacted several such legendary ancient voyages. In 1977, he built a replica of St Brendan's curragh and retraced his voyage to America.

However, the earliest evidence of travellers reaching America is to be found in ancient Chinese texts. Astronomers Hsi and Ho lived in China and travelled to America in 2640 BC. Studying their texts, scholars have concluded that Hsi and Ho followed the Asian and North American coastline before venturing inland to the Grand Canyon region and further south to Mexico and Guatemala. Shortly after their return to China, they failed to predict a solar eclipse and the Emperor Huang Ti had them executed.

Expeditions across the Pacific from Asia to America continued. Wixepecocha was a Hindu missionary who island-hopped across the South Pacific and reached Central America in about 400 BC. Evidence of this and other Hindu journeys is scant, but legends on both sides of the Pacific back up the theory. Hui Shun (458 AD) followed the path of the earlier Chinese astronomers and spent 40 years in Central America before returning to China. He is said to have named Guatemala in honour of Gautama Buddha.

In the eleventh century the Norsemen, or Vikings, made serious attempts to settle in America. They had settled in Iceland and Greenland and had ventured further to the New World. The first European born in America was a Viking child. The first record of Vikings reaching North America tell the story of Bjarni Herjulfson who, in 986 AD, was blown off course while attempting to visit his father in Greenland. He made his American landfall at what is modern-day Massachusetts.

Archeologists have discovered settlements in Newfoundland that confirm Vikings lived in the New World hundreds of years before Columbus. Greenland was well known to the Vikings and they had many settlements there. It was from Greenland that explorer Leif Ericson set out to find further lands to the west. His first landfall was on cold, rugged Baffin Island, not unlike Greenland with its mountainous ice floes and fringes of fertile soil along the coast. Labrador, on the mainland of North America, was also rugged but not quite as cold. Finally, Leif established settlements in an area he named Vinland. This was a place of abundant grain, timber and wildlife. This part of Canada is now called Newfoundland and the Viking settlements were unearthed in 1960.

After the winter of 1003–1004 Leif and his crew returned to Greenland and related their findings to their comrades. Several expeditions to America followed. Studies of ancient Norse manuscripts reveal that Vikings explored the American coast as far south as New York and maybe further. Seven years after Leif Ericson's first trip, his brother-in-law tried to settle on Vinland. They established camp for a while – long enough for a child to be born: Snorri Karlsefni, nephew of Leif Ericson. However, the aggressive Vikings were no match for the local Indians. After several fatal setbacks, the Vikings pulled out of America and lived on settlements closer to their homelands.

Other documents tell tales of Welsh and African trips across the Atlantic, but the most amazing story to emerge is about a Danish and Portuguese joint venture that discovered America just sixteen years before Columbus set sail. King Alfonso of Portugal and King Christian I of Denmark wanted to find a western sea route to China. Johannes Scolp and Joao Vaz Corte Real sailed from Denmark in 1476 and explored Hudson Bay and the St Lawrence river. But their short-sighted sponsors only saw what their men had failed to achieve. They hadn't found a route to China, and their reports about a possible vast new continent were ignored.

What all these tales prove is that who discovered America is not important – even Columbus thought he had reached Asia! – but what matters is the fact that the Spanish were prepared to grasp the opportunity presented to them by their explorer. Columbus is remembered today, not because he was the first to discover America, but because he discovered it for a people who acted on the information.

BURIED ALIVE

These events took place in 1837 in Lahore, India, and were confirmed by Colonel Sir Claude Wade, Dr Janos Honiberger and the British Consul at Lahore. A yogi named Haridas was entombed for forty days and forty nights. He was locked in a box, sealed in a pavilion and heavily guarded. Prior to the experience he made the following arrangements.

For many days he consumed only milk and on the date of his burial he ate nothing at all. Then he performed a yoga purification ritual involving the swallowing of a long cloth; this strip of fabric was left in his stomach and soaked up bile and other unclean substances in Haridas's body. It was then removed and the yogi placed himself in a deep, deep trance. His helper then "sealed" Haridas's body with wax. All openings were plugged and he curled his tongue to block his throat. The yogi was lifted into the box which was sealed and left in the pavilion which was also sealed.

After forty days, the body of the mystic was removed and his assistant washed him with warm water and massaged his head with yeast. He removed the wax, forced open his mouth and uncurled his tongue. The assistant anointed the yogi's body with butter and, after half an hour, Haridas was back to normal, walking around, none the worse for his ordeal.

WATCH OUT! HERE COMES ANOTHER FALLING BABY

Joseph Figlock lived in Detroit, USA. One day in the spring of 1975 he was walking along the street, alongside a high apartment block. A toddler on the fourteenth floor wandered close to an unguarded window and fell. Plummeting to earth, the baby was lucky to bump into Figlock, who broke his fall. Both Figlock and the baby survived the incident unharmed. In 1976, a different baby in a different apartment block fell to the street through an open window. For a second time Figlock was hit by a baby falling from the sky. For a second time both Figlock and child escaped unhurt.

THE IRISH AIRCRAFT DISASTER

On a clear spring day in 1968 an Aer Lingus Viscount plane disintegrated in midair during a routine trip. Flight 712 – code named Echo India Alpha Oscar Mike – was en route from Cork to Heathrow on Sunday morning, March 24. Between them, pilot and co-pilot had over 2,500 hours flying experience on Viscount planes. The flight was initially monitored by Irish Air Traffic Control at Shannon. At 11.32 am pilot Captain O'Beirne confirmed that he was travelling at 17,000 feet and had passed Tuskar Rock off the coast of Wexford. Everything was in order and the pilot confirmed that he would be over Strumble Head near Fishguard in about six minutes.

Air hostesses prepared to serve snacks to their Irish passengers and to some twenty Swedish tourists who were on the first leg of their journey home after a fishing holiday in Kerry. Two minutes later, Shannon

Air Traffic Control radioed the plane, telling him to switch frequency to London. Captain O'Beirne confidently repeated the message and confirmed the frequency that he had to switch to for London.

"Echo India Alpha Oscar Mike, with you." The message was picked up in London, but the London tower was mildly irritated because O'Beirne's message interrupted contact with another incoming plane. London Air Traffic Control expected Aer Lingus Flight 712 to repeat its message once the airwaves were clear. A mere eight seconds later a frantic message came: "Twelve thousand feet, descending, spinning rapidly!" Distorted screams could be heard in the background; after that there was silence. London tried in vain to regain contact.

The disabled aircraft plummeted into the sea just ten miles off the Irish coast, not far from Tuskar Rock lighthouse. What happened is unknown but it appears that, after disaster struck, the captain gained some sort of control of his craft and headed for Ireland. Maybe he vainly hoped that a crash-landing on a Wexford strand was possible. The craggy coastline of Wales spelled doom.

A German sailor thought he saw a bird plummet into the sea around noon and thought no more of it. Another Aer Lingus flight bound for Bristol scurried to the site of Oscar Mike's last message, hoping to see something. A hillwalker near Greenore Point saw a tower of water rising from the sea close to the lighthouse. A rescue operation was mounted within minutes, with helicopters and boats rushing to the Welsh coast. It was only when witnesses heard the story on radio or TV news bulletins that they realised what they had seen. On the following day, the search focused off Tuskar Rock. Some wreckage was sighted less than six miles from the lighthouse. Of the sixty-one passengers and crew, fourteen bodies were recovered. Nearly two months passed before the main body of the plane was located on the sea floor. It was lifted and brought to join the rest of the puzzle lying in a hangar in Baldonnel aerodrome.

On any Sunday morning, church bells rang announcing the times of various masses. Sunday, 24 March 1968 was no different. In the days that followed, many witnesses came forward, able to time what they saw or heard to just before or just after a particular church bell. No one remembered hearing the doomed plane passing over on a routine flight, but many heard strange sounds in the sky on that clear spring morning. "Like thunder," some people said. "Like rolling explosions in the sky," or "Loud crackling noises," according to others. Four different people claimed to have seen a red-winged high-speed craft with its tail "glowing like a fire". One witness saw this object darting through the sky and said it was followed by a loud bang.

What these people heard and saw is all consistent with an object breaking the sound barrier – the tell-tale sonic boom coming from a craft powered by a red-hot jet engine. These events happened in 1968, a full year before the commercial Concorde made her maiden flight. If the various witnesses are to be believed, the object they saw had to be military.

Was the innocent Aer Lingus plane mistakenly shot down by a supersonic missile? If so, was it part of a British training manoeuvre? Did it belong to NATO? Was it fired from a Russian submarine secretly patrolling the area? High-ranking Irish Government officials made their enquiries and drew a blank on every road they investigated. The most likely source of a stray missile was the British Ministry of Defence rocket range at Aberporth in Wales – but British officials assured Irish officials that the base was closed that particular Sunday.

Respected scientist and science fiction writer Arthur C Clarke would class Aer Lingus Flight 712 as a Mystery of The Second Kind: something which is unexplainable with current knowledge, but may be explained one day. Perhaps the answer lies buried deep in the archives of some defence organisation. Perhaps secret papers will be released in decades to come. Time will tell.

A DREAM – OR NIGHTMARE – COMES TRUE

In 1954 Eva Hellstrom, a psychical researcher in Sweden, had such a vivid dream that she wrote down a description of it. She dreamt that she and her husband were flying over a particular suburb of Stockholm and witnessed an accident. She saw a green train run into a blue tram. She wrote that the accident would happen when the train coming from Djursholm suburb hits the tram at Valhallavagen Street. Mrs Hellstrom even drew a sketch of the accident.

At the time of her dream there were no green trains in service in Stockholm. However, on March 4 1956, nearly two years later, the accident happened exactly as her notes and sketch described it. A blue tram was hit by a newly-commissioned green train.

THE 20-YEAR CURSE OF THE WHITE HOUSE

A bizarre series of tragedies have hit the White House, based on a twenty-year cycle going back to 1840.

Look at the years 1840, 1860, 1880, 1900, 1920, 1940, 1960. All the American presidents elected to office in those years died in office. Some died of natural causes. Some fell to assassins' bullets.

A triumphant William Henry Harrison defeated sitting President Van Buren in the 1840 election. Harrison was a well-known public figure after he had defeated the Indians in battle thirty years earlier. When elected president he won 19 of the 26 American states. His magnificent inauguration took place on March 7, 1841. This man, famous for his tough rugged campaign against the Indians in his youth, was not up to the chill wind that blew in Washington on that March morning. The president-elect stood on his podium and made the longest inauguration speech in history. He caught a chill during that speech and never recovered. He was dead in less than a month.

The man who was elected president in 1860 endured a turbulent historic presidency, steering his country through a bloody civil war. On 8 April 1865, the war ended when Confederate General Robert E Lee surrendered. On April 11, Lincoln made a speech urging all American people to work together in a spirit of reconciliation and reconstruction. Around this time Lincoln noted in his diary details of a strange recurring dream: "There seemed to be a deathlike stillness about me. Then I heard subdued sobs as if a number of people were weeping. I thought I left my bed and wandered downstairs . . . there was a corpse wrapped in funeral vestments. "Who is dead in the White House?" I asked of one of the soldiers (guarding the corpse). "The President," was his answer, "killed by an assassin." Then came a loud burst of grief from the crowd which woke me from my dream. I slept no more that night."

On the day of his assassination, Lincoln told one of his bodyguards about the recurring dream and the bodyguard urged the President not to go out to the theatre that night. Lincoln said that he had promised his wife that he would go. Unusually, though, on his way out, he said "Goodbye" to his White House bodyguard rather than his normal "Goodnight". Failed actor and bitter Southerner John Wilkes Booth sneaked into the Presidential Box at Ford's Theatre and shot the president in the back of the head. "The South is avenged!" shouted Booth as he leaped from the box and on to the stage. He broke his leg in that fall but escaped. He was hunted down and killed two weeks later.

James Garfield won his place in the White House in 1880. In July 1881, he was shot in the back by one Charles Guiteau. The assassin was a disgruntled hanger-on who had hoped to get a well-paid job in the new administration. The unfortunate President Garfield survived the attack for two agonising months before he died on 19 September 1881.

President McKinley was elected to a second term of office in 1900, but suffered the same fate as Garfield and was gunned down by a mentally unstable loner. This time it was a Polish-born anarchist named Leon Czolgosz.

By 1920, times were good in America. World War I was over, and the 1920s are remembered for good times and prosperity. President Warren G Harding was a relaxed, honest sort of man, best remembered for his game of golf and for all his corrupt cronies who took advantage of the gentle president. Harding died of a stroke in 1923.

The 20-year jinx has to be stretched a little in order to include President Franklin D Roosevelt. He served four terms, being elected in 1932, 1936, 1940 and 1944.

Stricken by polio in his youth, this wheelchair-bound president died of natural causes during the closing days of World War II in 1945.

1960 saw the election of the youthful, charismatic John F Kennedy. On 22 November 1963, Abraham Zapruder took an early lunch-break and strolled over to Dealy Plaza in Dallas, Texas. He owned a movie camera and he wanted to find a good place to capture a glimpse of President Kennedy and his beautiful wife Jacqueline as they passed by in a slow-moving presidential motorcade. To his horror he recorded the dramatic death of America's much loved President. Zapruder's experience was truly "stranger than fiction". If a novelist decided to write a story about the killing of a president, he would be stretching his reader's imagination too far if he had a cameraman who just happened to be there recording the most crucial moments of the story.

Has the 20-year jinx vanished? In 1980, journalists everywhere filled newspapers with the story. It was the year that Ronald Reagan was elected to office. At 68, Reagan was the oldest man ever to be elected president. Newspapers focused on his vice-president George Bush, placing him "a heartbeat away from the presidency". It looked like a prophesy come true when Reagan was ruthlessly gunned down in Washington by lone assassin John Hinckley in March 1981. However, Reagan survived not one but two terms as president of the United States. Although suffering from Alzheimer's disease, Reagan has survived to see two presidents serving in the White House after him.

Watch this space in the year 2000. No doubt the broken 20-year curse of the White House will be tossed around the papers and TV screens once more. Who will seek and who will win the office of the American presidency?

THE ANCIENT BATTERY

In Baghdad in 1936, railway workers toiled in the searing heat as they cleared the way for a new line. It often happens in the cities around the Mediterranean and the Middle East that workmen come across ancient sites. Then work has to stop and archeologists are called in to examine what has been found before work can continue.

The Iraqi workmen came across an ancient grave marked by a large stone slab. Work was interrupted for two months while authorities excavated the site. All the artefacts – beads, small figures, bricks, broken pottery and so forth – came from a period dating from 248 BC to 226 AD. In other words, everything was at least 1700 years old.

A curious object was found amongst the other artefacts: a copper tube with an iron rod lodged inside. It was passed on to Wilhelm König, a German scientist who worked in the Iraq Museum laboratory. This broad-minded investigator came to a startling conclusion. He was looking at an ancient battery – at least fifteen centuries older than existing theories of electricity.

The records don't show whether or not König managed to take the primitive electric cell back to Germany, but he did take his notes and compared his findings with other items lodged in the Berlin Museum. There he found similar cylinders whose purpose had never been worked out. There were clay jars with asphalt stoppers with the cylinders lodged inside. The cylinders were curiously corroded by some sort of acid. König concluded that as many as ten of these devices were used – linked together by bronze wires to create a stronger electrical current.

Why wasn't the scientific world taken by storm? These new facts didn't fit existing theories about the development of science. The ancient batteries were dismissed as a hoax. However, some hard-working, less pessimistic scientists brushed the dust off König's notes and agreed that our ancestors in Mesopotamia really did have electricity up to 2000 years ago. The wider scientific community still ignores these findings.

What did these ancient people use the electricity for? The most likely theory is that a series of these batteries were used to create a charge to electroplate a fine layer of gold or silver on to some other less precious metal. Is this likely scenario the real reason why the ancient battery story is hushed up? Are there museums around the world with valuable collections of "solid" gold and silver artefacts from ancient times which aren't so "solid" after all? Wouldn't it be in their best interest to keep the story of 2000-year-old electricity hushed up?

TELLING A LIE . . .

Deep in Papua New Guinea there are tribes who only recently have been exposed to the technology of the twentieth century. Could the following be an extract from an eye-witness account of helicopters landing in their remote valley?

". . . a stormy wind blew from the north, a great cloud with light around it . . . They were of human form . . . There was a wheel on the ground by each of them . . . when they went forward, the wheels went forward beside them and when they left the ground, the wheels left the ground . . . I heard the noise of their wings as they moved; it sounded like rushing water . . . "

That was not an eye-witness account of events in Papua New Guinea today. It was an account of something witnessed by the prophet Ezekiel in the Old Testament.

DISAPPEARING DINOSAURS

About 50,000 years have passed since Modern Man appeared on the planet. Dinosaurs reigned for about 160 million years. In other words, they have roamed the earth around 3,200 times longer than we have. In the grand timescale of geology, dinosaurs were wiped out more or less overnight. It is lucky for us that they became extinct. While those primitive monsters roamed the Earth, the puny ape-like animals which evolved into humans would have had no chance of prospering.

What happened? Why did the environment change so that it was no longer an advantage to be a big bully? Why was it suddenly more advantageous to be a small and nimble mammal that didn't have to eat as much? Dinosaurs lived during the Mesozoic Era, from about 225 million years to about 65 million years ago. Fossil records, layers and layers of sediment laid down over the years, tell us this. The oldest fossils are found in the deeper layers; newer fossils closer to the surface.

Gradual climatic changes don't fully explain the dinosaurs' disappearance. If conditions got warmer or cooler, dinosaurs would have had time to adapt and survive, just like smaller creatures. In fact, we are certain there were many climatic changes during the 160 million years that dinosaurs were around. These giant creatures survived all the ice ages of the period – ice ages are events that happen quite suddenly in a geological timescale.

The most significant clue in the mystery of the disappearing dinosaurs is iridium. This hard, brittle, steel-grey element is similar to platinum and is used in jewellery, watch bearings and in tiny high-tech scientific instruments. But what has iridium got to do with dinosaurs? This rare element is common in asteroids or mini-planets that wander through the solar system. Geologists digging through layers of sediment, deeper and deeper into the earth's past, have found lots of iridium in the 65-million-year-old layer. These deposits are found worldwide, not just at sites where fossilised dinosaur bones have been located.

Scientists reason that a huge meteor must have plummeted to earth 65 million years ago. Imagine a mushroom-shaped cloud following a nuclear explosion. Imagine all that energy multiplied a million times. This is a theory that many reputable scientists now hold. If a meteor a hundred miles across hit the earth, that's the kind of energy that would be released. The iridium-rich meteor would have disintegrated, scattering a dark dust-cloud right around the whole planet.

The earth would darken, temperatures would plummet, vegetation would shrivel up and animals depending on that vegetation would die. A dark, cold winter lasting several years would wipe out all but the most nimble and hardy of land creatures. Reptiles of the sea would have a better chance of survival. After the dust-cloud settled and the planet warmed up, sea creatures could gain a foothold once again and tread along the slow path of evolution once more.

That's probably what happened. A huge impact crater called the Manicouagan crater exists in Quebec, Canada. It is 60 miles across, but scientific dating techniques show that the impact happened long before the 65-million-year-old layer of iridium was laid down.

For many years scientists feared they wouldn't find enough evidence to support their "crashing meteor" theory. It was possible, after all, that the meteor had landed in an ocean. However, in the jungles of Central

America, the outline of a 110-mile-wide crater has recently been confirmed. The age of the crater has also been confirmed – it is 65 million years old. The mystery of the disappearing dinosaurs edges closer and closer to a solution.

TIME OF DEATH – PREDICTED ACCURATELY

It takes one human lifetime for Halley's Comet to complete its orbit of our solar system. Every seventy-six years this twenty-mile-wide dirty snowball skims past our sun, warms up and amazes us with its spectacular tail. The comet appeared in 1835, the year that American author Mark Twain was born. Twain often stated that he had come to this life with Halley's Comet and that he would leave this life when the comet came back for him. Twain kept his promise; when the comet reappeared in 1910 the old man of letters died.

JEANE DIXON AND THE KENNEDYS

"The Vietnam war will end in ninety days." "Russia will invade Israel." "China will use germ warfare against America." These are just a few examples of predictions which American psychic, Jeane Dixon, got wrong. Although Jeane Dixon used a crystal ball, she wasn't the Madame Zsa Zsa type; she wasn't a gypsy wearing a shawl, peering into a crystal ball sitting on a velvet tablecloth. Jeane Dixon's husband was in real estate and very wealthy. She had several fur coats and carried a crystal ball in her handbag. She was a Christian, believed in God and went to church.

Jeane Dixon told Winston Churchill that he would lose power after the Second World War and would

28

regain it in 1952. The great leader did not believe her but events happened exactly as she said. She predicted the suicide of Marilyn Monroe and that UN Secretary-General Dag Hammarskjold would die in a plane crash.

While in church in 1952 she had a vision of a blue-eyed, brown-haired man standing in front of the White House. The date 1960 was etched in front of him. Once she had witnessed the complete vision, Jeane Dixon passed on upsetting news to her friends. A Democrat, she said, would be elected president in 1960 and would be assassinated while in office. It saddened Dixon when the first part of her prediction came true and John F Kennedy was elected. If that event had come to pass, surely the murder of the great man was bound to happen as well? Returning to church many times, she prayed that her prophecy was wrong.

Sadly, each time she gazed into her crystal ball she saw a dark cloud hovering over the White House. Early in 1963, Jackie Kennedy gave birth to a third child, Patrick, a brother for Caroline and John Jr. Sadly, in the summer of 1963 the infant died. This incident helped console Jeane Dixon's friends. They were certain that the dark cloud hanging over the White House in Dixon's crystal ball marked the tragic loss of the little infant. But Jeane Dixon maintained that the cloud was not connected with young Patrick. She still believed that President Kennedy would die in office.

When the dark cloud in the image descended on the White House, Dixon was distraught. It was November and there was talk of the president visiting Dallas. The psychic felt strongly about that trip: the president must not go. She had to warn him. Jeane Dixon was a wealthy, privileged member of society who knew people who knew the Kennedys. She made arrangements to meet Kay Halle from Cleveland whose father was a friend of John F Kennedy.

"Tell the president not to make his trip to the South," she urged. "He must not go. He will be killed."

Kay Halle did not doubt Jeane Dixon's sincerity and anguish but she couldn't bring herself to pass on the message. Even if Kay had no doubts of her own, she was certain that the Kennedys had no time for psychics and mystics. President and Mrs Kennedy made the trip to Dallas, unaware of Jeane Dixon's prediction.

On Friday, 22 November, 1963 Dixon met a friend for lunch in Washington. She was troubled and had no appetite. Suddenly there was an uproar.

"Kennedy's been shot!" somebody cried. There was a radio in the kitchen.

"He's dead," Dixon said.

"No! Just wounded. That's what the radio said."

Half an hour after those shots rang out in Dealey Plaza, Dallas, John F Kennedy died.

During the following year Jeane Dixon had another disturbing vision, featuring the late president's younger brother, Teddy. She saw a crash involving a small plane. Frantically she tried to get word to Teddy to warn him to stay away from private planes for at least two weeks. There was no time to get the word to the young Kennedy. On the day after Dixon's prophecy, Teddy Kennedy broke his back in a plane crash.

Word of Jeane Dixon's powers spread and she was invited to speak on radio and TV shows. She was most famous for her predictions concerning the slain president. In 1968, another presidential campaign was in full swing and Senator Robert Kennedy was the leading Democratic contender.

While speaking at a seminar in the Ambassador Hotel, Los Angeles, a member of the audience asked Dixon if Bobby Kennedy would become the next president of the United States. Suddenly in Dixon's mind a black curtain came down between her and the crowd. Shaken, she answered the question:

"No, he will not. He will never be president because of a tragedy that will take place right here in this hotel."

A week later, on 5 June, Senator Robert Kennedy was in the Ambassador Hotel celebrating his win in the Californian primary election. As he left the hotel, walking through the kitchen, he was gunned down, and he died the following day.

A MILITARY FUNERAL FOR A HORSE

A horse belonging to an Irishman survived Custer's Last Stand at the Battle of Little Big Horn. Captain Myles Keogh, originally from Leighlinbridge, County Carlow, was killed alongside General Custer and 224 other soldiers. Keogh's horse, Comanche, was so badly injured that the Sioux Indians didn't bother stealing him. Troops discovering the carnage of the battlefield came across Comanche with seven horrific wounds, including a punctured lung. The horse was saved and pampered for the rest of his life. After his death at the age of thirty, Comanche's insides were given a military funeral while his carcase was stuffed. Comanche's final resting-place is in a humidity-controlled glass case in the University of Kansas Natural History Museum.

HITLER AND THE HOLY LANCE

Many have heard of the legendary Holy Grail, the chalice that Jesus used at the Last Supper. Lesser known, but equally significant, is the Holy Lance – used by an unknown Roman soldier to pierce Jesus's side as He hung on the cross. Three institutions claimed to have the original Holy Lance: one in Paris, one in the Vatican and one containing the Hapsburg Lance in Vienna.

The weapon that eventually became known as the Hapsburg Lance was discovered in Antioch by crusaders during the Middle Ages and carried back to central Europe. German folk legends claim that the emperor Charlemagne carried it on his various military campaigns. Saxon King Heinrich carried the Holy Lance as he drove Polish settlers from the eastern fringes of Germany. The ruthless 12th-century conqueror Barbarossa possessed the lance when he conquered Italy.

The lance passed into the hands of the Hapsburg royal family and rested in a museum in Vienna.

While a down-and-out artist in Vienna in 1913, Adolf Hitler was already a man obsessed by the occult and with a warped sense of his own destiny. He had learned about the Hapsburg lance and was enthralled by it. He told a colleague, "I slowly became aware of a mighty presence around it. I sensed a great destiny awaited me, and I knew beyond contradiction that the blood in my veins would one day become the folk spirit of my people." He was consumed by the religious, military and Germanic significance of the history of the Hapsburg Lance.

In 1938, close to the peak of Hitler's powers, the triumphant German Chancellor announced at a rally in

Vienna that he was making Austria part of the Nazi Empire. As Hitler spoke, his soldiers were already at work seizing the Holy Lance and other Hapsburg treasures. These were brought to St Catherine's church in Nuremberg, the spiritual heart of Hitler's Nazi movement.

Less than eighteen months after the seizure of the Holy Lance, Hitler plunged Europe into World War II. At first, the ruthless dictator was lucky and appeared invincible. Later, as the war ended and his empire crumbled around him, Hitler still believed his destiny was to be victorious. Allied forces rumbled in from the west; the Soviets stormed Berlin; but Hitler was still convinced that he would miraculously gain the upper hand. In October 1944, the city of Nuremberg was bombarded both from land and from the air. Instead of evacuating innocent civilians, Hitler ordered that the city be reinforced. He moved the Holy Lance and other treasures from St Catherine's to a reinforced vault.

On 20 April, Hitler's 56th birthday, Nuremberg finally fell to the Allies. Captured German prisoners of war told guards how Hitler had squandered the lives of thousands of men in the hope of securing the Holy Lance. Ten days later, American Lieutenant William Horn's men discovered the vault amid the rubble of the ruined city. He presented the Holy Lance to his commanders and, to this day, it remains the property of the United States Government. That date, April 30th, the day his enemies took possession of the Hapsburg Lance, was also the day Hitler ended his life with a bullet from his pistol.

THE DESERTED LIGHTHOUSE

Lighthouses hold a popular place in our imagination. They are pillars of security and outposts of danger. Men have braved treacherous seas to build towers and to light beacons to guide travellers of the sea. The round tower is the best shape to withstand the fury of stormy seas. Once sailors see a lighthouse, by day or especially by night, their position on the sea is confirmed. They know where they are; they know where they are going.

In the last century, many British ships were lost off the north coast of Scotland and a decision was taken to build a lighthouse on Oileán Mór, the largest of the Flannan Islands, about seventeen miles west of the Hebrides. The project was ambitious; the Northern Lighthouse Board allowed two years to build their lighthouse on the rugged, distant rock. In the end, it took four years to haul building materials and equipment to the top of the 200-foot cliff. Two jettyies were built on the island, one to the east and one to the west. The idea was that one jetty would always be sheltered from the buffeting storms.

The lighthouse was opened in December 1899. Nearly a year later, ten days before the first Christmas of the new century, the light failed to come on. Three experienced lighthouse keepers were posted on the island – Ducat, MacArthur and Marshall – but this was in the days before radio contact. Fierce storms raged. The two jetties offered no protection to any rescue team daring to cross the open choppy seas. It was 26 December 1900 before a rescue party, under the command of a Captain Moore, was able to leave the mainland and investigate. They carried Christmas presents for the men, hoping against hope that things were all right and there was a simple explanation for the light going out.

As they got closer to the lighthouse the would-be rescuers waved their semaphore flags, looking for a response from one of the three guards. There was none. They moored at the eastern jetty and climbed the steep steps to the lighthouse. The door was closed but unlocked. Cold ashes lay silently in the grate. The clock had stopped. At this lower level, there were no signs of the three keepers. Captain Moore took three sailors with him as he ascended the stairs within the tower. Not knowing what to expect, he pushed open the door of their sleeping quarters. Everything was tidy, the beds were made and nothing appeared to be amiss. The hardened sailors were frightened. All of them knew the tale of the deserted *Marie Celeste* where the crew had vanished nearly thirty years previously.

The lantern at the top of the tower was primed and ready to light. There were ample quantities of oil and a neatly-trimmed wick was in place. Downstairs, Captain Moore found slates where lighthouse master James Ducat had kept records. The last record was made at 9.00 on the morning of 15 December. Everything appeared to be in order. It had been a calm day – but that night the lantern had not been lit, signalling a mystery that remains unsolved today. A dejected Captain Moore and his crew left Oileán Mór, returning with the keepers' unopened Christmas presents. Two days later a panel of expert investigators sailed out and tried to piece together the puzzle.

A crane at the western jetty had been damaged; tangled ropes were wrapped around the hoist, about sixty feet above the waterline. A toolchest normally lodged in a crack in the rock had been washed away. Could a hundred-foot wave have thundered against the cliff, washing away the three keepers and the toolbox? More importantly, could this have happened on a day when one of the keepers had recorded conditions as being "calm"? If such a freak scenario had occurred, why were all three experienced men washed to their doom?

It looked like damage to the crane was suspected and two of the keepers went down to have a look. Two sets of oilskins were missing from the men's quarters; a third was found hanging on a hook on the wall. Maybe the first two keepers were caught off guard, had time to scream, and the third raced out to help, not having time to pick up his oilskins. Standard life-saving equipment like lifebelts and ropes remained intact. Whatever happened to the three men on that calm day in 1900, no clues were ever found to enable the investigators to solve the case.

THE $27.50 LIGHT BULB

How many Chicago electricians does it take to change a light bulb?

One. But he charges $27.50.

True. It happened at the McCormick convention centre in Chicago. Orderlies used to get $47 an hour for taking computers out of boxes. They couldn't plug them in, though; electricians had to do that. Faced with competition from other big American cities, union people in Chicago have relaxed their rules. Nowadays, exhibitors at the convention centre can change their own light bulbs or plug in their own equipment.

GRISLY CROCODILE ATTACK

One of the most horrific true stories to emerge from World War II concerns the gruesome fate of nearly one thousand Japanese soldiers. Conditions in Southern Asia for both British and Japanese soldiers were harsh. They had to fight in heavy, damp heat and hack their way through dense jungles. The Japanese seemed to have the upper hand. They were used to hot, humid summers in their homeland and they had a better knowledge of what to eat and what not to eat in the jungles.

On 19 February 1945, troops were in the middle of an incident on an island in the Bay of Bengal where the British had the advantage. They were fighting a band of about one thousand Japanese and had the back-up of heavy British artillery. Darkness fell and the Japanese were cornered in swampland. Some were wounded, others dead, but the able-bodied Japanese were prepared to fight their way out of their corner the following day.

Scenting blood in the air and in the water, huge crocodiles descended on the helpless troops. All night long, the British cringed as they listened to their helpless foes screaming in the dark. At dawn they found that there was no enemy left to fight. Fewer than twenty Japanese soldiers survived the frenzied crocodile attack that lasted the entire night.

THE HAZARDS OF ARMY LIFE

During the period from 1983 to 1988, thirty-nine American servicemen were injured and five were killed in bizarre circumstances where the servicemen were actually the aggressors. Who were the objects of this aggressive behaviour which led to serious and fatal counter-attacks? The victors in all the cases referred to were – vending machines! Soldiers attacked the machines in the hope of shaking out free drinks or of revenge after one of the menacing machines had eaten their coins without supplying a drink. The deaths and injuries occurred when the machines fell on the servicemen.

THE PALACE GHOSTS OF VERSAILLES

On a shaded lane once used by French queen Marie Antoinette, two English ladies stepped back into the past. Charlotte Moberly and Eleanor Jourdain were tourists, sauntering through the magnificent gardens at the palace of Versailles. The year was 1901 and the two ladies lost their way while heading to a small private mansion not far from the main palace.

The air became heavy. The women felt dazed and moody. Afterwards, they said that they seemed to be sleepwalking. Both of them saw peasants wearing old-fashioned clothes going about their business outside their humble cottages. Two men wearing green were obviously gardeners. They had an old wooden wheelbarrow and several antique tools. The tourists asked these men for directions to Marie Antoinette's private palace and they sent them further into the woods.

Both women remember that there was something uncanny about the scene. The trees looked like cardboard cut-outs. A cloaked man stared at them from within a little kiosk, something like a bandstand. The two tourists crossed a rustic bridge and emerged into an English-style landscaped garden. From there, they could see the small mansion they were looking for. The building was closed but a lady sat on the terrace drawing a picture. As they walked around the building, a footman greeted them and invited them to stroll around a French garden before he brought them inside the building. The two English ladies witnessed a wedding party and their curious mood lifted. They were comfortable and enjoying themselves again.

Later on, as they talked about their afternoon, it transpired that they both had different accounts. Miss Moberly remembered some incidents; Miss Jourdain remembered others. Both ladies came to the conclusion that they had experienced some kind of apparition and decided to write down their accounts. They were both educated women, not inclined to believe in ghosts.

They returned to Versailles the following year and were astonished by what they saw. Rusty locked gates blocked the path they had taken. There were no stone cottages and a garden was covered with a gravel path. Rhododendron trees with several years growth were rooted in the ground where only the previous year peasants seemed to be going about their business. Now lemonade stalls thrived and tourists were everywhere.

In 1901, the two Englishwomen not only saw ghosts but claimed to have been shipped spiritually back to another time. They entered rooms which had been locked for decades. They saw agricultural tools that were no longer used. The two women were so astonished by their adventure that they decided to do more research and write a book on their experiences.

Simply titled *An Adventure,* their book has been a

source of much controversy ever since. Maybe the women had stumbled across a fancy-dress picnic; maybe the peasants were actors rehearsing a new play. These kinds of suggestion were followed up but proved fruitless.

The most convincing proof that something profound happened to the two English ladies was found in some old maps. When writing up their experiences, they described the layout of the paths taken and bridges they had crossed. They positioned the old cottages and the little landscaped gardens they had stumbled on. Several years after their accounts were written down, maps were found that showed the layout of the Versailles gardens in Marie Antoinette's time. The details on these maps corresponded with what the two tourists had described.

Charlotte Moberly and Eleanor Jourdain were convinced that, on that hot August day in 1901, they had stepped back more than 112 years and entered the world of the doomed queen Marie Antoinette.

THE CURSE OF TUTANKHAMEN

Lord Caernarvon financed the archeological dig that led to the discovery of Tutankhamen's tomb. Three months later, he was bitten by a mosquito and an infection set in. At precisely five minutes to two on the morning of April 5 1923, he died. At the same moment two other events occurred: in England the Lord's dog howled and died and the city of Cairo in Egypt suffered a blackout.

UNIDENTIFIED FLYING OBJECTS

Do unidentified flying objects exist? The answer is "possibly". However, because so much nonsense has been written about flying saucers and the like, it is nearly impossible to separate believable stories from the hoaxes. If UFOs appear in remote areas, we dismiss the stories as hoaxes created by lonely oddballs to relieve their boredom. If somebody sees a UFO over Central Park, we dismiss the claim because nobody else can back up the tale. (The boxer Mohammed Ali claims to have seen a craft like a huge electric light bulb in the sky while he was jogging in Central Park in 1972.)

Take away the isolated sightings where there are no other witnesses, and take away the UFOs from populated areas where there *should* be more witnesses, and we are left with a core of sightings which might make the grade; sightings made by sensible people and backed up by independent witnesses. Believe it or not, serious UFO researchers do their best to debunk all the claims that come their way. Nearly nine times out of ten, researchers do manage to dismiss UFO reports. New military planes, weather balloons, comets, meteors, cloud formations and even flocks of migrating geese have been mistaken as unidentified flying objects. Most sightings can be rationally explained. However, about ten per cent of sightings have to be classified as mysteries. At Dr J Allen Hynek's Illinois Centre For UFO Studies, over 50,000 unexplained cases are jammed into his database; some of these follow.

The Roswell Incident

A report in New Mexico's *Daily Record* dated Tuesday 8 July 1947 carried the following headline: "Air Force captures flying saucer on ranch in Roswell region". On the night of 2–3 July, rancher Bill Brazel couldn't sleep as wind and rain raged outside in the worst storm New Mexico had experienced in years. In the middle of his tossing and turning, Bill heard an explosion. At daybreak he saddled up and headed out to make sure that his sheep were all right and to investigate the strange explosion.

His fields were covered with slivers of black timber and shards of flat metal. The "wood" was extremely light and would not break or burn. The foil-like metal would not fold or dent. Some scraps had strange hieroglyphics engraved on them. Not far away, the rancher came across a large battered object, disc-shaped and obviously the source of the debris.

Bill Brazel wanted to believe that he was looking at a secret prototype plane from the nearby Roswell airfield. Then he came across the motionless remains of "the crew". None of them was human. They had small eyes, large heads, small bodies and wore one-piece metallic grey uniforms.

The frightened rancher galloped home and notified the sheriff who, in turn, alerted the nearby airfield. This incident happened less than two years after the atomic bomb was dropped over Hiroshima and the Roswell airbase was home to the 509th US Air Force Bomb Group, the only combat-trained atom bombers in the world. The wreckage on Bill Brazel's farm, whether it was Russian or extraterrestrial, indicated a possible threat to America's national security.

After the army investigated, they wanted to hush up the incident and swore Bill Brazel to secrecy. However, the local gossip machine spun into top gear. On 8 July, without the authority of his commander, the Roswell Base public information officer issued a press release as follows: "The many rumours of the flying disc became a reality yesterday when the intelligence office of the 509th Bomb Group gained possession of a disc through the co-operation of some local ranchers."

International news services picked up the story and the Pentagon was furious. The original story was denied and an alternative "weather balloon" yarn was released to the media. The authorities successfully cooled down the media frenzy and it was rumoured that the alien craft, along with the bodies of six aliens, was quietly shipped deep to top secret military bases across the United States.

Papua, New Guinea

On 26 June 1959 something happened at Fr Gill's Boianai Mission in Papua, New Guinea. Taking a stroll after dinner, he noticed the planet Venus shining brightly. He also noticed that there was a strange new light hanging in the sky just above the familiar planet. The longer he looked, the clearer the image became. The priest wasn't looking at one bright light, but several. They hovered above the gathering clouds, causing them to glow. In full view of thirty-eight witnesses, four human-like figures emerged from one of the objects and began carrying out some task.

The whole episode lasted about three hours and took place at an altitude of less than 2,000 feet. The priest took careful notes of what happened and twenty-five adults, including teachers and medical assistants, signed his report.

Similar events occurred the following night, lasting about an hour. Fr Gill wanted to dismiss the sightings as American or Australian flying machines, but neither group could explain what the priest and his community had seen. The quality of the priest's notes, plus all the extra witnesses, baffled authorities. No man-made machine was capable of making the clouds glow as they did and no man-made machine could hover over one spot in total silence.

The Missionary Nun

When priests, nuns or other religious folk tell strange stories they are usually taken seriously. However, nearly 400 years ago, an eighteen-year-old nun told a tale so bizarre that not even her Mother Superior believed her. Sister Mary, from a small convent in Agreda, Spain, claimed she had been flown to Central America where she converted a tribe, the Jumano, to the Christian faith. She said that during the flight she had seen the entire earth spinning below her. Sister Mary got off lightly: she wasn't burned for heresy, but her diaries were destroyed which was a pity because, a few years later, a series of events surfaced which gave credit to her story.

Fr Alonzo de Benavides was sent to the New World to do some missionary work. In 1622 he wrote home to the pope and to his king, complaining that he had been sent to convert the converted. The tribe he was in touch with already knew how to celebrate Mass and they already had rosaries and crucifixes. They claimed that a lady in blue had taught them and had given them their religious objects. Neither pope nor king knew anything about a female missionary sent to the area.

After returning to Europe in 1630, the priest heard about the claims of Sister Mary. He went to Agreda to investigate. Fr de Benavides was stunned when the humble sister was able to give accurate descriptions of his Indians and their villages. She knew local folklore that no outsider could possibly have known. The convent superiors were baffled. And, to cap it all, the priest produced a chalice that the Indians had. It was identified as one that had disappeared from the Spanish convent years ago.

The American President's sighting

In 1973, the Governor of Georgia was Jimmy Carter, who would later become president of the United States. After an official dinner, Carter and twenty other guests were sitting on the verandah of a residence in Thomastown, Georgia. All of them saw a disc that was about the size of the moon. They gazed in awe as the UFO switched from red to green and back again.

After becoming president, Carter sanctioned $20 million for the study of UFOs.

HOUDINI

Born in Budapest in 1874 a little boy named Ehrich Weiss learned how to pick locks so that he could steal his mother's apple pies. He used to impress visiting circuses with agile rope tricks. After his family moved to America he worked at several jobs, including time served as a locksmith. This young man wanted to become a magician. Deeply impressed by accounts of the life and exploits of French magician Jean Robert Houdin, Weiss changed his name to Harry Houdini. In time, he became the most famous magician ever.

In his lean days, Houdini and his wife Bess tried lots of variations on their act just to keep bread on the table. At this time their most successful act was a complete sham based on spiritualism. People always want to make contact with the "other side". They want proof that they really go somewhere after they die. Houdini and Bess would go to a new town, slip a few dollars to local talkers and get information on their potential audience. Then they would set up a mind-reading session. They'd rattle off a few facts they picked up and the crowds would be enthralled.

On one level, the Houdinis laughed at how easy it

was to fool their audience. On another level, they were deeply concerned at ordinary people's willingness to be taken in by ruthless tricksters. After he achieved fame as an escape artist, Houdini spent a lot of his life unmasking fake spiritualist mediums.

Harry Houdini was a devoted husband and son. No matter where he was, he always sent money to his widowed mother. After her death, Houdini's interest in spiritualism took on a new twist. As well as using his talents to expose tricksters, Houdini hoped that he would find a genuine medium and use that person to contact his dead mother. He contacted medium after medium but never found a person capable of passing his stringent tests. Often Houdini would visit his mother's grave and mourn his failure to contact her.

17 June 1922 was the anniversary of his mother's death. On that day, Houdini was involved in a seance with a certain Jean Doyle, wife of Sir Arthur Conan Doyle, creator of Sherlock Holmes. Mrs Weiss "spoke" to her son during this seance and Houdini was, at first, very moved. He was certain that people of the Doyles' standing were sincere but, the more he thought about his experience, the more he doubted what had happened. His mother spoke only broken English but the woman speaking through Lady Doyle spoke perfect English. The Doyles genuinely felt that contact had been made, but Houdini remained sceptical. The issue caused a rift between the friends.

Although both were interested in spiritualism, Houdini and Doyle had different approaches. Houdini did his best to unmask the cheats; the writer always tried to give mediums the benefit of the doubt. Later on, Sir Arthur Conan Doyle claimed that Houdini himself was the greatest medium alive – able to transform himself into a spirit in order to escape from locked boxes!

Houdini died in 1926 after a student hit him in the stomach in order to test the magician's strong muscles. Houdini had not braced himself for the blow and died of a burst appendix several days later. The Houdini-the-spiritualist tag remained with him. Every year, on the anniversary of his death, his admirers gather at his grave hoping for a sign from the other side. Year after year they have seen and heard nothing. As Houdini himself once said, "Anyone can talk to the dead, but the dead do not answer."

THE DISTURBED BURIAL VAULT

A wicked slave owner named Thomas Chase is not allowed to rest in peace – neither are members of his family. They lived in Barbados in the Caribbean and the following sequence of uncanny events begins in 1812. Dorchas Chase, daughter of Thomas, died in July 1812. Her death was caused by a slow, suicidal starvation – a way, she thought, of escaping her father's cruelty. It was decided to bury her in a vault which was already occupied by a Mrs Goddard and a baby.

A month later, old Thomas Chase himself died and the funeral cortège made its way to the vault in the grounds of Christ Church, Barbados. It took eight men to move the heavy stone slab lined with lead which guarded the entrance to the vault. Their lamps illuminated the heavy darkness inside and, to their horror, they came across a scene of mayhem. Dorchas' coffin was tossed on its side; the baby's coffin was upside down. Mrs Goddard's coffin was untouched, resting snugly on its own shelf.

The slave owner's family assumed that the damage was caused by disgruntled slaves who hated the master of the family. There were no signs of forced entry, but the family talked themselves into believing their own story. The negroes who had helped carry the coffin to the vault were edgy, though. With their customs of voodoo and African legends, they suspected black magic. They tidied up the vault, put the coffins in their place and laid Thomas Chase to rest – or so they thought. The vault was resealed and the edges of the heavy slab were given a generous coating of cement.

Four years later, the tomb had to be opened for another family burial. The cement seal was intact and there was no other way to enter the vault. The coffins, however, had moved. The mourners convinced themselves that they had just forgotten the exact resting-places which they had laid out for their relatives four years earlier.

In 1819 the vault had to be opened again. The cement was chipped away but the stone was nearly impossible to move. Extra men and horses were called in to move the slab and, once they were inside, the reason for the blockage became obvious: the coffin of old Tom Chase had been wedged against the door of his own tomb. The other coffins were tossed around. Yet again, Mrs Goddard's coffin remained undisturbed.

Lord Combermere, Governor of Barbados Island, was puzzled. There had to be an explanation for the mystery, he reasoned. Before the vault was resealed, he ordered sand to be scattered on the floor of the vault. Beach sand from the Caribbean has a texture like talcum powder. It is not the grainy sort of sand that covers many beaches. Even the slightest disturbance would be recorded on this dusty coating on the floor of the Chase family tomb.

After eight months, Lord Combermere and some dinner guests were curious. Had the tomb been disturbed again? They hadn't the patience to wait for another family death before opening the tomb. They were eager to rip open the vault themselves. In the name of law and order, Combermere decided that the vault should be examined.

The seals were broken and the door was opened. A handful of witnesses gazed inside. All the coffins, except Mrs Goddard's, were scattered again. The fine sand on the floor was unmarked. There were no footprints. There were no scraping lines caused by dragging heavy coffins. There was no explanation.

Frightened, the Governor ordered all the coffins to be buried elsewhere. The vault has been empty ever since.

Detectives, geologists and local priests were unable to come up with a rational explanation for the eerie events. The area is prone to volcanic tremors and earthquakes, but there had been no such events during the period in question. Even if there had, why wasn't Mrs Goddard's coffin disturbed? Maybe the water table had risen and had floated some of the coffins to new positions? Impossible: slave owner Thomas Chase's coffin was made of lead; the undisturbed Mrs Goddard had been laid to rest in a wooden coffin.

The frightened negroes of the island were the only ones with a hint of a solution. Somewhere from the depths of their voodoo culture, a spirit rose and caused the mayhem.

THE LOCH NESS MONSTER

Note: This file was obviously compiled by a non-believer in the Loch Ness phenomenon. Read on.

During the hot shimmering summer of 1933, a Mr and Mrs McKay were driving home in Scotland. Mist floated on the road before them. They opened the windows of their car to allow some of the breeze to take away the sleepy heat. They admired the sunshine as it sparkled and danced on nearby Loch Ness. To their astonishment, they saw a large whale-like animal plunging and rolling in the water. They rubbed their eyes in disbelief. They mentioned the incident to a few friends and one of them must have sold the tale to a newspaper. After a couple of weeks, the *Inverness Courier* picked up the story. Soon many others came forward claiming to have seen something.

By sheer volume, Loch Ness is the largest British Lake, larger than Lough Neagh and Lough Erne put together. Its relatively small surface area masks the fact that Loch Ness is very deep. It is about twenty miles long and a mile wide, but up to 950 feet deep. That's plenty of dark, deep murky water in which a monster can hide.

The story in the local paper was soon relayed nationwide and it caused a sensation. One article had the comment: "If this thing is as big as they say, it's not a creature, it's a monster." And so the legend of the Loch Ness Monster was born. A year later, a London surgeon named Robert Wilson became one of the first of many tourists to visit the region. On April Fool's Day, 1934, he took a photo which astounded the world. Looking like a submerged swimmer's arm stretched skywards, the photo has baffled experts ever since. Doctor Wilson seemed to have captured, on camera, the infamous Loch Ness Monster.

To enrich the story, researchers found out that St Columba had seen the monster back in 565 AD. While St Columba was crossing the Loch in a boat, the monster apparently followed him. The saint made the sign of the cross and told the monster to go away. It did, reappearing again in that hazy summer of 1933.

Curious tourists have booked bedrooms in local hotels ever since. One of them, Anthony Shiels, took another clear picture of the monster in 1977. He said that the animal was greyish-brown with a paler underside. Its skin texture was smooth and glossy. It held itself very upright before it sank very smoothly beneath the surface. Shiels added, "I am sure Nessie appeared as a result of my psychic powers."

In time, the story went worldwide and American money flowed into the area. Ultrasound, underwater photography and other technologies were employed to map the depths of the loch. No monster and no suitable hiding-places were found. In 1972, while under the threat of being closed down due to lack of funds, the Loch Ness Phenomena Bureau released a hazy photograph of the entire body of an underwater creature, complete with a narrow neck, a whale-like belly and a tail. It looks like Nessie has a sense of humour, appearing to the Bureau researchers just as they were about to pack up after ten years of – nothing.

Let the final word be given to celebrated naturalist Sir Peter Scott, the son of Sir Robert Falcon Scott who perished near the South Pole in 1912. During the 1980s, when interest in the Loch Ness monster was at a peak, Sir Peter named the creature *Nessiteras Rhombopteryx*. His attention to the Loch Ness mystery gave the whole issue credibility. When his official Latin name for the monster was circulated, interest soared. After many weeks, an observant TV commentator noticed that *Nessiteras Rhombopteryx* was an anagram of "Monster Hoax By Sir Peter S".

CORK WOMAN TAKES DOWN NOTES FROM THE DEAD

Cork woman Geraldine Cummins could take dictation at the rate of 1500 words per hour. In the

1920s, unseen spirits spoke to her as she sat at her desk. After a few weeks, she had taken down notes which accumulated to over a million words. She wasn't too impressed with what she was hearing, though. It was all heavy, biblical stuff, giving details of the further travels of St Paul and Barnabas. The narrator spoke in glowing terms about St Paul. Geraldine was not too fond of the work of St Paul because of the anti-feminist attitudes he had. Anyhow, day in, day out, Geraldine Cummins took down this dictation and the manuscripts were finally made into a book called *The Scripts Of Cleophas*. Readers and critics were impressed. The richness of detail was such that the book read as if written by someone who had actually lived in the first century AD. Some religious commentators said that the work could be a lost section of the Bible, detailing the little-known period between the death of Jesus and Paul's departure for Athens.

Who dictated this stunning book to the Cork woman? Whoever "wrote" the book had in-depth knowledge of Greek, Latin and Hebrew cultures and languages. Born in Cork in 1890, Geraldine Cummins was the daughter of a Professor of Medicine who lectured at University College, Cork. One of eleven children, she had literary talent long before the mysterious voice dictated *The Scripts of Cleophas* to her. She wrote two novels and had short stories published in British magazines.

Many people, on hearing the background to her biblical novel, came looking for personal messages from relatives who had passed on. Cummins often stunned her clients with the words she hurriedly wrote down. Often the pages would contain private and personal details known only to the deceased and their living relative.

When Geraldine Cummins lived in London,

Canadian prime minister Mackenzie King looked her up and arranged seances. On one of these visits, the late president Franklin Roosevelt passed on a message to King, telling him about DeGaulle's eventual rise to power in France and about the imminent Korean War.

Cummins was also useful to the Irish writers Sommerville and Ross. Violet Martin of Ross used the pen name Martin Ross and collaborated with Edith Sommerville to create the successful Irish RM books. After her death, Violet Martin appeared to continue writing – using the hand of Geraldine Cummins. So, the Sommerville and Ross partnership continued. Edith Sommerville insisted that the name Ross appear alongside hers on books completed long after the death of Violet Martin of Ross.

Her experiences with Sommerville and Ross, with *The Scripts of Cleophas* and with many other lesser-known souls, convinced Geraldine Cummins that there was life after death and she died a happy woman in Cork in 1969.

MEN OF PROPERTY

What did the following American presidents have in common: George Washington, Thomas Jefferson, James Madison, Andrew Jackson, Zachary Taylor, John Tyler, James Polk, Andrew Johnson, Ulysses S Grant?

They were all slave owners.

How about American patriot Patrick Henry who, during the American War of Independence, said the unforgettable "Give me liberty or give me death"? He owned 65 slaves.

Future president Ulysess Simpson Grant was the general who defeated the Confederates in the American Civil War. This conflict led to the freeing of all American slaves.

BODY IN A BOTTLE - SORT OF

Charles Coghlan was an actor and a man of the world. Born in 1849 on Prince Edward Island, Canada, he came to fame as a Shakespearian actor in London. He travelled internationally with his acting troupe, but always considered Prince Edward Island to be his home. Whenever he could manage it, he spent time in a holiday home which he purchased close to the village where he was born.

While on tour he died in Galveston, Texas, in 1899. In those times it was impossible to consider shipping his body back to his beloved island and he was buried locally. Less than a year later, a hurricane lashed against the coast of Texas, killing thousands and reducing acres of property to rubble. Floodwaters mercilessly ravaged cemeteries, carrying coffins into the Gulf of Mexico. Many of them sank nearby or were washed up on the Texas shore. Coughlan's coffin, however, drifted across the Gulf and around the tip of Florida. There it was caught in the northbound Gulf Stream and made its way along the Atlantic coast of America.

Once the coffin was caught up by the forces of the ocean in this way, it should have continued all the way to Ireland or beyond. However, it must have encountered another storm off the coast of Newfoundland because the strange box was discovered by fishermen off the Canadian coast in 1908.

These fishermen happened to be from nearby Prince Edward Island and they tossed out their nets to haul in their find. Scraping barnacles from the box, they discovered the silver coffin plate bearing the name of their local hero, Charles Coghlan. His remains were brought to shore just miles from the village where he was born. Coghlan was reburied in the local cemetery.

MESSAGE IN A BOTTLE – TWO

In 1934 Doyle Branscum stuck his photo in a bottle and tossed it into a river in his native Arkansas. From there, the bottle made its way south and into the Gulf of Mexico. It was 24 years before the bottle washed up on the shores of Florida. It was predictable enough that the currents should carry Branscum's photo to Florida, even though it was odd that the straightforward journey should take so long. Even more strange, however, was the fact that the bottle was picked up by one Bill Headstream, an old school-friend of Branscum.

THE MILLENNIUM TIME BOMB

"... 1996, 1997, 1998, 1999, 1900, 1901, 1902 ... "

Wait a minute! doesn't 2000 come after 1999? If you are a computer, the answer is probably "no". In fact, computers don't recognise the "19" at all. When it comes to recognising dates, they have been programmed to recognise the last two digits of the year. We read 31/12/97 as being December thirty-first, nineteen ninety-seven; the computer reads what's there – and there's no "nineteen". The computer also knows that the next date in the sequence is 01/01/98.

On January 1 in the year 2000, the computer will think it has gone back in time by a hundred years.

There's an interesting story about a time-lock in a bank vault. It's controlled by a computer chip embedded in the twenty-tonne door. For security reasons, the computer chip won't allow the vault door be opened on Saturdays or Sundays We couldn't have potential thieves fiddling with the chip and helping themselves to what's in the vault over the weekend, now could we? Of course, there's a bank built on top of the vault – more security.

On Friday, New Year's Eve, 1999 the chip in the vault door will read 31/12/99. Next day, Saturday, January first, 2000 the door will think it is 01/01/00 which, back in 1900, was a Monday. Therefore the vault will be open on the first Saturday and Sunday of the year 2000, but will remain closed later in the week when it thinks it is the weekend.

The chip is so well embedded in the 20-tonne door that the only way of gaining access to it is by removing the door; and the only way to get heavy equipment down to remove the door is to remove the bank first. All to replace a wafer of silicon, smaller than your little fingernail, that wasn't programmed to recognise the year 2000!

How about the inboard computer in a sophisticated German car that lets you know you are due for a service? Suppose the driver gets everything checked out in 1999 and isn't due back to the garage for a year. Next January, from the computer's point of view, the car hasn't been serviced for a hundred years. The computer will shut everything down so the negligent driver can't do any more harm.

Cameras, digital watches, video recorders . . . everything with a built-in electronic clock will be affected. Time is running out. All the software engineers have inadvertently programmed computers to tell us "The end of the world is nigh!"

A MAN, A DATE, A SHIPWRECK

On 5 December 1664, a ship sank with 81 passengers on board. There was one survivor, a man named Hugh Williams.

On 5 December 1785, a ship sank with 60 passengers on board. There was one survivor, a man named Hugh Williams.

On 5 December 1860, a ship sank with 25 passengers on board. There was one survivor, a man named Hugh Williams.

DO WE HAVE AN IRISH LOCH NESS?

Note: Please read the note written underneath the title of the Loch Ness Monster file.

On Wednesday, 18 May, 1960 three priests went fishing on the banks of Lough Ree on the river Shannon. Father Dan Murray, Father Matt Burke and Father Dick Quigley had brought refreshments with them and they were relaxed, pleased with their day out, happy that the waters were so calm. Lough Ree has a habit of turning rough and dangerous without much warning. On that warm May evening, their peace was disturbed, not by a storm brewing, but by a large unidentified animal swirling in the water just one hundred yards from them. The large flat-headed animal swam towards the priests. The three astonished men jumped to their feet. The head and neck of the animal stood about two feet out of the water, but most of the animal remained beneath the surface. The priests were unable to see whether the strange creature used legs or flippers to propel itself along.

There is supposed to be a *Peiste* or lake monster in the small Lough Fadda in Galway. Captain Lionel Leslie, a cousin of Winston Churchill, heard about the rumours and went exploring in a very unscientific way. In October 1965 he blew up a few sticks of dynamite beneath the water. Something came to the surface and floated lifelessly, just fifty yards from the shore. Captain Leslie was convinced that his experiment with dynamite had uncovered a monster. Rather than investigating further and ruling out the possibility that the object might be a lump of wood or a stunned otter, the good captain retreated to the local pub to report his findings to his colleagues.

Fishermen often have stories about the "one that got away". A schoolteacher who fished on another Galway lake in 1962 told a story about a monster that got away. He was happily fishing in the lake when, suddenly, his line went taut. The teacher claimed that he had hooked a creature the size of a cow. It had short, thick legs and its grey skin was covered in bristles. The teacher also claimed that the animal had a face like a hippo and with a horn like a rhino's. Given that fishermen are prone to exaggerate, the teacher's "cow" was probably a hairy, bristly otter holding a silver fish in its mouth. Imagine the schoolteacher returning to the village with nothing to show for his day on the lake. A strange monster makes for a better tale than a six-inch trout.

SPONTANEOUS COMBUSTION

Spontaneous combustion – what a way to go, being burned at the stake without a stake. Spontaneous combustion happens in nature all the time. Wherever dead vegetation builds up, bacteria deep inside the mound can ferment and give off heat. If the fermentation process is rigorous enough, enough heat is generated to set fire to the mass of rotting vegetation.

Workers in a garden products factory near Hacketstown, County Carlow have to watch out for this problem all the time. Trucks carrying tree bark are delivered to the site and the small factory grades and slices the stuff into mulch for garden use. During their busy season, little hills of bark accumulate, waiting to be processed and packed.

On Easter Sunday 1997, two units of the local fire brigade dashed to the site. The smouldering mounds of bark had caught fire and the entire factory was in danger of going up in smoke. Once the fire was extinguished, one unit of the brigade remained on stand-by for three days just in case spontaneous combustion struck again before the workers had a chance to spread out and cool down their raw material.

Can the numerous reports of living people bursting into flames be explained? Some can by reference to the abuse of alcohol or tobacco. But if the plausible tales of accidents or carelessness are filtered out, a core of unexplained spontaneous combustion cases remain.

In the 1960s, Don Gosnell had a regular job reading gas meters in Coudersport, Pennsylvania. One of the clients on his route was his old family doctor, John Irving Bentley. Aged 92, he was retired, but still able to look after himself despite being a semi-invalid. He shuffled around his old house with the help of a walking-aid. On an icy cold winter's morning, 5 December 1966, Don Gosnell arrived to read the doctor's gas meter. The front door was unlocked, but that was not unusual in the small community where everybody knew everybody else. "Hello, Doc! It's me, Don! I'm here to read the meter." He called. Although he got no reply, Don made his way down the familiar steps to the basement where the gas meter was located. There was an odd smell, like burnt oil from a brand new central heating system. He sniffed and noticed a subtle, wispy blue cloud hanging in the air. A small cone of ash lay on the floor, probably the source of a little fire since gone out. Casually, he kicked the pile, read the meter, and went back upstairs.

Gosnell was still slightly concerned about the doctor and decided to go into the old man's living-room. There was nobody there but the smoky smell that lingered in the house was stronger. There was still no sign of the doctor. The visitor entered the nearby bathroom which was over the basement where he had read the meter.

Minutes later, breathless and as white as a sheet, the

panicked Gosnell was back in his office, just able to mutter four words: "Doctor Bentley burnt up!"

Back in the bathroom, there was grisly evidence of a bizarre case of spontaneous combustion. The doctor's scorched walking-aid leaned against the bathtub. A hole had burned all the way through the floor to the basement below. The pile of ashes that Gosnell had casually scattered earlier that morning were the remains of the old doctor. Not all of the doctor's mortal body was consumed in the mysterious fire. Lying on the bathroom floor was a leg, severed just above the knee by the scorching heat. The doctor's right foot still nestled snugly within his slipper.

On 2 July, 1951 a Mrs Carpenter of St Petersburg, Florida woke up and was alarmed by the smell of smoke coming from her neighbour's apartment. She went over to Mrs Reeser's place to investigate. She knocked on the door, and when she got no reply, tried the door handle. It was too hot to hold. She went for help, found a few workmen and forced the door open. A gust of hot air burst into the corridor. Inside, a charred human body, some burnt furniture springs and a pile of blackened ashes were discovered. Investigators were baffled. If Mrs Reeser had been the victim of a nasty accident, why were some parts of her body reduced to ashes that even a $2500^{\circ}F$ crematorium could not produce? And how was it that the only damage to the apartment was contained within a four-foot blackened circle?

Then there was James Hamilton, a professor of mathematics in Nashville, Tennessee, who survived a weird happening. On a winter's day in 1835, he felt a searing pain in his leg. Looking down, he witnessed a six-inch flame leaping from his trousers. Hamilton slapped his leg in vain to extinguish the flame, but many agonising seconds passed before he managed to cup his hands around the affected area and starve the fire of oxygen. Could the cause have been a stray cinder from a hot chestnut vendor? Unlikely. The burn on his leg took a long time to heal; a hole had been burnt into his underwear, but in his outer trousers there was no hole at all, just a scorch mark from where he had killed the flame.

In Italy in the 18th century, a "yellowish, utterly loathsome half liquid smoke" oozed from the windows of the Countess Di Bandi's bedroom. Her remains were discovered four feet from her bed and her legs, with stockings on, remained untouched. Nearly all of the rest of her body was reduced to ashes and soot floated around the room. Neither the furniture nor the floor were burned but two candles nearby had melted.

"'Look at my fingers!' . . . A thick yellow liquor defiles them, which is offensive to the touch and sight and more offensive to the smell. A stagnant sickening oil with some natural repulsion in it that makes them both shudder . . . It slowly drips, and creeps away down the bricks . . . lies in a little thick nauseous pool . . . And the burning smell is there – and the soot is there, and the oil is there – and he is not there! . . . There is very little fire left in the grate, but there is a smouldering suffocating vapour in the room, and a dark greasy coating on the walls and ceiling . . . it is the same death eternally – inborn, inbred, engendered in the corrupted humours of the vicious body itself, and that only – Spontaneous Combustion, and none other of all the deaths that can be died."

The death of the miser Krook, in
Chapter 32 of *Bleak House*
by Charles Dickens.

NATIVE AMERICANS - WELSH SPEAKERS

In the late 1700s, a story about two Welsh missionaries spread through London. They had tried to convert North American Indians to Christianity. One particular tribe were not interested and they captured the two men and sentenced them to death. As they thought about their fate, the two missionaries mourned to each other in their native Welsh tongue. Their captors were astonished; the Indians understood Welsh! The Indians set the missionaries free. The story was taken seriously by a Welsh druid named Iolo Morganwg who tried to put together an expedition to search for the "Welsh" Indians. Morganwg, himself was ill and couldn't make the trip. His friend, John Evans, went in his place. Evans discovered nothing and died in New Orleans.

Old manuscripts recorded the story of the Welsh-speaking Indians and the adventures of a Welsh prince named Madog who is said to have landed in America twice during the late 1100s. He is supposed to have built his first settlement in 1170. Then he went home, leaving a colony of 120 Welshmen behind him. When he returned in 1190, he found that all the settlers had been slaughtered. Madog himself died in America soon afterwards. The location of the site of Madog's settlement may be in Florida, Alabama or the West Indies; the accounts differ. It was traces of Madog's settlement that the Morganwg-Evans trip hoped to uncover in the late 1700s.

AREA 51

Not everybody who lives in Las Vegas works in a casino or hotel. Some scientists who live in the suburbs regularly take a short plane-hop to Area 51 research centre. Area 51 is not just a location in the blockbuster movie *Independence Day*. Area 51 actually exists. It is a military research base, and whatever goes on there is a closely-guarded secret.

The little town of Rachel (pop. 150) is the closest civilian settlement to the secret base. Highway 375, which goes through the town, has signposts naming it "The Extraterrestrial Highway" because of all the unexplained sightings that have been made in the area. The base is probably developing high-tech military aircraft, but the military are not saying, are they? It is likely that some of the stranger sightings made nowadays are merely advanced fighter planes that will become well-known (or obsolete) in ten years' time.

Tourists and investigators sometimes wander off the Extraterrestrial Highway and head up the dusty track to Area 51. In the middle of nowhere they are greeted by a sign which reads:

It is unlawful to enter this area without permission of the installation commander.

Sec 21. Internal Security Act of 1950; 50 USC 797.

While on this installation all personnel and the property under their control are subject to search.

USE OF DEADLY FORCE AUTHORISED

There is no fence at this point, just the sign. The fence is located a quarter of a mile further in, out of sight over the next ridge. The military are playing a clever game. If people pass by the sign and stroll up to the sentry box at the fence, they are arrested on the spot. After all, they had disobeyed the sign by entering the area beyond it without permission. By not having the sentry box and the fence at the outer edge of Area 51, the guards on duty don't have to be hassled by investigators and reporters standing just inches outside the restricted area.

Meanwhile, back in Rachel the community is buzzing with UFO activity. The local *Desert Rat Newsletter* is devoted entirely to the mysterious goings-on at Area 51. The editor, Glen Cambell, sells the paper mainly to tourists and he also acts as a guide to anybody who wants to be taken to nearby hills outside the restricted area but overlooking Area 51.

If aliens ever did crashland in North America, Area 51 is the ideal secret location for the authorities to bring the wreckage for secret examination. Who knows? Maybe aliens did crash in the Nevada desert. Maybe modern high-tech US aircraft copy features which scientists picked from alien wreckage. It is unlikely that we will ever know, because the authorities are not saying. If you try – and fail – to penetrate Area 51, you can always go back to Rachel and enjoy a cola in the local "Little A'Le'inn".

HITLER AND STALIN

During World War I, the battle of the Somme dragged on and on. French and German soldiers faced each other from their trenches, separated only by the barren, exposed no-man's-land between them. In this damp, rat-infested mucky place a Bavarian corporal woke in a cold sweat having had a horrific dream. He had seen himself buried alive in his trench. Crumbling earth and molten metal poured down upon him and he felt the moisture of his blood soaking his tunic.

When he woke, he seemed to be safe. There was no activity in his own trenches nor from the darkened French trenches opposite him. However, the dream had disturbed him and he stepped out of his trench into the eerie calm of no-man's-land. There was no cover between himself and his French opponents. He was prone to be hit by stray bullets or shrapnel from either side. The corporal knew this and the rational part of his mind told him to return to the relative safety of his own trench. However, he kept going, deeper and deeper towards the centre of no-man's-land, further from his own lines.

Suddenly a French offensive began and the corporal fell to the ground. Shells and bullets whined overhead as the frightened German kept his head covered. He heard a massive explosion and, after a while, the French ceased firing. Cautiously, the corporal made his way back to his original position. A vast crater filled the site of his old trench. His comrades were dead or dying; some of them were buried alive by the French onslaught.

The name of the Bavarian corporal who was saved by a dream was Adolf Hitler. Already a believer in the paranormal, Hitler was convinced that he had a special mission in life and that a great destiny lay ahead of him.

Needless to say, Hitler retained a special interest in the paranormal after his brush with death. During World War II, stories of a stage mind-reader disturbed Hitler. Wolf Messing predicted the dictator's death if Hitler "turned to the East". Hitler put a price on the Polish mind-reader's head but Messing escaped to the Soviet Union.

In Russia, Messing came to the attention of Stalin. The Russian tyrant set a test for the mind-reader. Could Messing enter Stalin's country house, even though the guards and secret police weren't told to expect a visitor? The test was too easy. Messing convinced the guards that he was Lavrenti Beria, the ruthless head of the Secret Police. The fact that the mind-reader didn't remotely look like Beria was irrelevant.

Stalin concocted another test for Messing – he was to rob a bank by telepathy. In due course he strolled into a bank in Moscow and handed a teller a blank piece of paper. The teller "read" the blank sheet and dutifully stacked 100,000 roubles on the counter. Messing walked out of the bank and confirmed what had happened to Stalin's two observers who were waiting outside. Once the astonished observers took note of what had happened, Messing went back to return the money. The befuddled teller took back the money and re-examined the paper with Messing's instructions. Seeing the paper to be blank, the poor teller had a heart attack – but survived.

THE FRIENDLY THEATRE GHOST

The Theatre Royal in Drury Lane, London is reputedly haunted. Joe Grimaldi was the original 'Joey the Clown' and his ghost had appeared regularly since his death in 1837. Theatre management were once offered an exorcism to get rid of the ghost and they flatly refused. Why? Because Joey is a good-luck ghost, bringing cheer to the actors and picking out winning shows. Joey saunters around wearing a sword, a three-pointed hat and a powdered wig. He is either wearing a theatrical costume or he is comfortable in the outfit of a late 18th-century gentleman.

He is not a spirit of the night. He usually appears during rehearsals but has also been known to show up for matinee performances. Sometimes he walks slowly through the stalls; sometimes he sits for a performance, only to disappear through the wall afterwards. King George VI came looking for the famous ghost, but the spirit declined to appear.

The ghost's appearance is considered to be a lucky omen

because he usually appears at rehearsals of shows that go on to be successful. Rogers and Hammerstein shows – *Oklahoma, Carousel, The King and I* and *South Pacific* were all particularly well liked by the Theatre Royal Ghost.

In fact, the ghost gave stage direction to a young actress named Green Duke as she rehearsed for *The King and I*, leaving her relaxed and better able to perform on her stressful opening night.

DEATH AT THE CIRCUS

7,000 people attended a performance of the Ringling Brothers and Barnum & Bailey circus in Hartford, Connecticut. The date was July 6, 1944. A fire broke out and 168 persons were killed. One victim, a girl aged about six, was not identified. Her face was unmarked and the police issued a photo of her when nobody came forward looking for her. The photo was circulated locally and then throughout the entire US. Days, months and weeks passed. To this day no relative, playmate or neighbour has ever come forward to identify her.

FLYING OVER PERU

The Pan-American Highway stretches from Alaska to the southern reaches of Argentina and Chile. As it winds its way across Peru, it cuts through the flat, featureless Nazca desert. This part of the highway was laid during the 1920s. Engineers, surveyors and workmen laboured in the area. From time to time they came across straight furrows or lines of small boulders. The workers were impressed by the ancient Inca Indians, who were able to lay such perfectly straight lines. But they also knew of the Inca city Macchu Picchu, higher in the mountains, where Inca engineering and precision stonework left admirers breathless. After Macchu Picchu, straight lines in the desert were no big deal. The engineers bulldozed their "straight line" highway across the desert, pushing sections of Incan handiwork out of the way.

In 1927, the road building team acquired additional tools to help them in their task: three old planes were used to help them map the best route across the desert. It was only from an altitude of three thousand feet that they realised the lines on the desert formed patterns. Climbing to six thousand feet, the surveyors gasped in astonishment. They looked down at criss-crossing lines, a humming-bird, a whale, warriors, animals and insects – all drawn with uncanny precision, marked out with furrows or lines of stones.

To the aviators in the sky, the straight lines looked like an airport, but why would an ancient culture who didn't even have the wheel need an airport? Later studies and excavations revealed the secret of the straight lines. They acted as an ancient calendar, lining up with the sun or stars on significant dates of the year.

Scientists spent years carefully brushing away centuries of desert sand revealing the patterns in their original splendour. After solving the riddle of the straight lines, several questions remained. Why were the various figures etched in the desert? How did the Incas draw their lines and images with such uncanny accuracy? Why make patterns that are only visible from high altitudes?

That last question raises the most theories, both credible and crazy. Could it be that the Incas were visited by beings who arrived from outer space? Could the patterns mean "Welcome, please come again"? Numerous books have been written about the possibility of aliens landing on the Nazca desert, but level-headed scientists continue to search for more rational explanations.

During the 1940s, German-born Maria Reiche spent several years excavating and cataloguing the area. Her conclusion was that the various symbols were simply for adornment. Once the Incas had managed to lay down their straight-line star calendar, they added beauty, just like they did to many artefacts they used. She became convinced of this theory when she worked out how the ancient people managed to lay down their patterns.

Working with Indians who had lived all their lives in the area, Reiche discovered countless dried-up wooden pegs hammered into the barren desert or already removed by the Indians. On the desert floor these marked the beginning or end of different lines, or points where the direction changed, or pivotal points for curves. She concluded that once the Incas had mastered straight lines, they pushed their skills to the limit, adding more and more complicated patterns. According to Reiche, they made scale models of what they wanted and then directed hundreds of labourers to lay down the patterns.

There was no need to conclude that visitors from the sky had landed in ancient Peru. People from every culture looked skywards and imagined their gods out there, looking down at them. The Incas did not have to see the patterns themselves to justify them – or did they? An American, James Woodman, studied the area and came up with chunks of evidence that suggested that the Indians used hot-air balloons. Patterns on pottery fragments looked like rafts hanging from spheres. The charred remnants of bonfires and ovens were found at the ends of some lines. Scraps of ancient fabric were so tightly woven that they could have retained hot air without it leaking through. Using local reeds and weaving cloth in the ancient way, Woodman did in fact build a working hot-air balloon that could have been built centuries earlier.

Surely, therefore, the lines and patterns of the Nazca desert are not a mystery at all? Aren't they just another monument to the skill and ingenuity of the human mind? Just because we are blinded by the technology and advances of the twentieth century does not mean that earlier peoples could not have been inventive.

THE DELTA JET

Made from solid gold, this little model has the delta-shaped wings of a modern fighter jet, an upright triangular tail and a little cockpit up front. Found in South America, this artefact is pre-Columbian and is, in fact, at least one thousand years old!

JIGSAWS - CONTINENTAL DRIFT

Question: What moves as fast as a growing fingernail and causes volcanoes and earthquakes?

Answer: The continents.

Long, long ago all the landmasses of the earth huddled together as one sweeping continent. Vast cracks existed in the deep rocky plates upon which the land rested. Inside the planet, a molten gurgling core of superheated magma sent currents of energy to the surface, not unlike the swirling patterns that can be seen in a saucepan of boiling milk.

Now, after 200 million years of drifting, geologists find evidence of their theories everywhere. The Appalachian mountains of the United States are geologically identical to the highlands of Scotland and the coastal ranges of Norway. Close relatives of animal species found in Madagascar, off the coast of Africa, turn up in India and South-east Asia. The unique and wonderful collection of odd animals that exists in Australia can be easily explained. Long ago on the evolutionary chain the continents were drifting and Australia was cut off; there was no land-bridge between Australia and other continents.

The highest mountain ranges of the world can be explained by huge ancient continents hammering into each other. India was known as the subcontinent long before the theory of continental drift ever existed. Millions of years ago, the vast landmass of present-day India was indeed a continent in its own right. Following its own course on a rocky plate, India eventually collided with the bigger Asian continent. The pressure of one landmass crunching against another forced the land upwards where they met. Today we see the result as the Himalayan mountain range. Thousands of feet above sea level, scientists are finding the fossilised remains of creatures that roamed the sea before the continents crunched together. Similar evidence can be found in the Rocky mountains of North America and in the Alps of Europe. The magnificent scenery of Switzerland today was caused by Italy pushing against the underbelly of Europe.

The single ancient continent was named *Pangea* – "all earth" by a German adventurer-meteorologist, Alfred Wegener, who first put forward his theory in 1915. He called the northern section of this great continent *Laurasia*. This area eventually split up to become present-day North America, Europe and northern Asia.

71

He called the southern part *Gondwanaland*, comprising today's South America, Africa, India, Australia and Antarctica.

Can the average reader "prove" the theory of continental drift for his or herself? The answer is "yes". Trace a copy of the map of the world and cut out all the different landmasses. Cut out India and the island of Madagascar and treat them as separate continents. What you have in front of you are the components of a curious jigsaw. Straight away, you will see that the east coast of South America fits snugly into the west coast of Africa. Less obvious is the match between North America and North Africa. Juggle with the pieces until New York sits a few hundred miles south of the Canary Islands and the continental shapes match pretty well. Match the west coast of Madagascar with the east coast of Africa, and the east coast of the island with the south-west coast of India. Antarctica locks in pretty neatly with Africa, India and the southern coast of Australia. The connections aren't perfect, of course. Over millions of years the pieces of the jigsaw have been battered by other forces, including erosion, ice ages and so forth.

This section opened with a question about the moving continents causing volcanoes and earthquakes. There are well known hot spots and danger spots all over the world. By matching known earthquake and volcano zones with the theories about what is happening underneath, scientists confirm that the continents are still moving. Volcanoes occur where there are weaknesses in the underlying crusts; magma oozes through the cracks and gushes to the surface. Earthquakes happen as chunks of the planet, having pressed against each other for centuries, suddenly slip, releasing vast quantities of energy and causing different areas on the planet's surface to slip apart.

The distance between New York and Rome is two metres greater today than it was in 1900. This drift continues and scientists have various sophisticated ways of measuring it – including laser readings taken from machines planted on the surface of the moon!

PULLING MY LEG

In 1976, builders working in Cornwall found a human arm attached to part of a ribcage. The decomposed body parts had been neatly sawn off. Instead of reporting their grisly find to the police, the workers left the remains high up on their rented scaffolding, along with a note reading: "In case you need a hand . . ." In due course the work was completed and another team of workmen came to dismantle the scaffolding. They treated their gruesome find in a similar manner and simply left it on a roadside. Eventually, a passer-by notified the police. Forensic examination took place, but the condition of the arm and ribcage was such that age could not be determined. The body parts were anything between five and one hundred years old. The case is still unsolved.

THE DEVIL'S FOOTPRINTS

In February 1855, people in a area of Devon, in south-west England, locked their doors against the devil. Overnight a series of hoof-like prints had mysteriously formed in the snow. Brave men armed with pitchforks and guns set out and followed the strange "Devil's Trail". The prints could have been caused by a normally-shod horse if, and only if, the horse had only one leg and could walk through brick walls.

On the night of February 7–8 the prints peppered the snow with machine-like accuracy. Generally they followed a straight line. If a practical joker was responsible, he would have had to carefully place one foot directly in front of the other and would have had to keep up the charade for more than forty miles. Before fear set in, the curious from Topsham, Devon, followed the tracks. When the prints stopped at a brick wall, the investigators scurried around the long way and picked up the trail at the far side of the wall. Curiously, there were no scuff marks going up or down the wall and the snow-capped ledge on top was undisturbed.

Sometimes the one-hoofed creature approached peoples' doors, but appeared to change its mind. The tracks wandered over a large patch of south-west England, across streets and fields, sometimes across stacks of hay – up, over, and down, never compressing the hay beneath the dusting of snow.

When the national papers picked up the stories, several experts and quacks had a field day with their unbelievable or silly theories. Maybe a one-legged kangaroo left the trail? The print didn't match a kangaroo's. How about the mark being, not a footprint, but the entire body mark of a small animal? That theory caught people's imagination as they imagined a frenzied hare or rabbit hopping across the landscape. Plausible, if the tracks had eventually taken the shape of a recognisable trail of a small animal running away. Not even a small fox would have the stamina to hop non-stop over forty miles.

Were the "footprints" planted by some airborne device which bounced some sort of contraption off the ground as it floated over? The theory is not as crazy as it sounds. Scientists at the time were experimenting with balloons, gathering information on air flows and the weather. Could one of these devices have broken loose and, as it gradually came to earth, left a print caused by a shackle hanging from the balloon? Every modern child who has played with a helium balloon knows that a time comes when the balloon withers and the string dangles along the ground. There is, however, a problem with the balloon theory as well. Witnesses reported and records confirm that the winds on that early February morning blew in an east-west direction. The pattern of the devil's hoofprints made a near circular pattern in the landscape.

The mystery of the prints in the Devonshire countryside will forever infuriate investigators of the strange and bizarre. The mystery is insoluble because it happened so long ago. It is tantalisingly evident that the mystery would be solved if the same clues were offered to the scientists of today.

THE COW JUMPED OVER THE MOON - ALMOST

In the film *Twister* there is a scene where a cow is sucked up by a tornado. A Guernsey cow named Fawn survived such an incident in 1962. In Iowa, USA, the animal was taken into the air and landed safely in a neighbour's pasture over half a mile away. Before her owner came to collect her, Fawn managed a brief affair with the neighbour's Holstein bull and produced a healthy calf the following year.

Five years later, a bus-load of startled tourists saw a tornado-borne cow floating through the air. It was Fawn, and once again she managed to land safely on all four hoofs.

Fawn became a celebrity and was a fairground attraction for many years. There was no more flying for Fawn, though. Every time a storm warning was issued, the venerable cow was safely locked in a barn. On 25 July, 1978 Fawn died peacefully at the ripe old age of 25.

THE MEATH MEDIUM AND THE BURNING AIRSHIP

Eileen Garret was born in County Meath on St Patrick's Day, 1893. As a child growing up in Ireland she heard voices and claimed to have invisible friends in her garden. This convincing, sincere lady moved to England and became one of the most respected mediums of her day. This lady always welcomed any scientific inquiry into her powers.

On 7 October 1930, Eileen Garret conducted a seance in London. Her colleagues hoped she could make contact with the writer Sir Arthur Conan Doyle, creator of Sherlock Holmes, who had recently died. The seance began smoothly with Garret receiving messages from various unknown souls on the other side. An Australian journalist, Ian Coster, was present at the seance and remained sceptical.

Sir Arthur Conan Doyle was not contacted that afternoon, but something very strange did happen . . .

Voices coming from Eileen Garret's mouth gave a frightening message, cloaked in all sorts of technical engineering terms. A man calling himself Irving or Irwin used Garret's voice to speak to the people gathered for the seance. "Fuel injection bad . . . gross lift computed badly . . . too much for engine capacity . . . failed to reach cruising altitude . . . airscrews too small . . . " The erratic voice went on and on, brimming with technical descriptions and details of a journey that ended in disaster.

Soon the people at the seance realised they were listening to somebody who had been involved in a very recent air disaster. Britain's pride and joy, an airship named the *R-101*, had crashed in France just two days before this seance. The hydrogen-filled airship was on its maiden voyage and forty-seven people were killed when it burst into flames in French fields near the town of Beauvais. The man in charge had been a Captain Irwin. All the papers had carried the story of the ill-fated airship, but the Australian journalist realised that Garret was giving them far more detailed information than she could have picked up from a newspaper. Ian Coster prepared a test for Eileen Garret. He asked for some more private seances where she would again contact members of the airship crew. She readily agreed to his request.

During these sessions the medium passed on messages from Captain Irwin and the Director of Civil Aviation, Sir Sefton Brancker, who had also perished in the disaster. These two men were anxious to let people know what had gone wrong. They urged authorities not to take foolish risks in the name of national pride. The *R-101* had been built amid a blaze of publicity, with the press following the story every step of the way. The authorities had been forced to set a deadline for her maiden voyage and known design flaws had to be hushed up so that the deadline could be met.

The Australian journalist was astonished by the wealth of information and technical detail being relayed through the voice of Eileen Garret. Speaking about the experience years later, he said that he simply forgot that Eileen Garret was in the room with him. He took his notes and listened to the two dead aviators as comfortably as though he were sitting with them in the lounge of a gentleman's club.

Eventually, Ian Coster's notes were taken for closer examination to the Royal Airship works in Bedfordshire where the ill-fated *R-101* was built. Engineers studied them and were astounded. Many of the details were surrounded in technical jargon and several industrial secrets appeared in her notes. Captain Irwin would have been familiar with those details, but there was no way Eileen Garret or any civilian could have known about them.

Is there only one possible explanation for the mystery surrounding the *R-101* and Eileen Garret? Has she really the ability to communicate with people who had passed away? She astounded scientists and sceptics alike. The story of Captain Irwin and the *R-101* is typical of many inexplicable contacts that Eileen Garrett made during her lifetime.

THE STRANGE WORLD OF GIANT SEA MONSTERS

Here is a word for word sea monster account, written in his ship's log in 1860 by Captain William Taylor, master of the British Banner:

"On the 25th of April, in Lat. 12 deg. 7 min. 8 sec., and Long. 93 deg. 52 min., E., {That's in the Indian Ocean, south-east of Java}, with the sun over the main-yard, felt a strong sensation as if the ship was trembling. Sent the second-mate aloft to see what was up. The latter called out to me to go up the fore-rigging and look over the bows. I did so, and saw an enormous serpent shaking the bowsprit with his mouth. It must have been at least 300 feet long; was about the circumference of a very wide crinoline petticoat, with black back, shaggy mane, horn on the forehead, and large glaring eyes placed rather near the nose, and jaws about eight feet long. He did not observe me and continued shaking the bowsprit and throwing the sea alongside into a foam until the former came clear away of the ship. The serpent was powerful enough, though the ship was carrying all sail, and going at about ten knots at the time he attacked us, to stop her way completely. When the bowsprit, with the jibboom, sails, and rigging, went by the board, the monster swallowed the fore-topmast, staysail, jib, and flying jib, with the greatest apparent ease. He shoved off a little after this, and returned apparently to scratch himself against the side of the ship, making a most extraordinary noise, resembling that on board a steamer when the boilers are blowing off. The serpent darted off like a flash of lightning, striking the vessel with its tail, and striving in all the starboard quarter gallery with its tail. Saw no more of it."

While we will never know for certain what Captain Taylor saw, it was most likely a giant squid. Creatures like octopuses, only much larger, have been documented. In 1893, part of the carcase of such a creature was washed ashore in St Augustine, Florida. Measurements were taken and tissue samples were sent to Washington for examination. Many years later it was confirmed that the remains found on the beach in Florida were from the octopus family. Taking scales from the scant measurements available, scientists determined that the intact creature would have had a tentacle span of over 200 feet.

Captain Taylor, in the Indian Ocean, estimated his creature to be 300 feet long. The horn he referred to could have been the parrot-like beak that such creatures have for tearing the flesh of their prey. The observation that seems to confirm that Taylor's creature was a giant squid is the creature's method of propulsion: "The serpent darted off like a flash of lightning". Squids propel themselves by squirting out liquid and moving forward, rather like a balloon moving forward as it loses air. This is probably what the sea captain saw on a giant scale.

FOREIGN LEGION GHOSTS

Hidden deep within the records of the French Army is the strange story of two dead Foreign Legion soldiers in Algeria, North Africa. Rene Dupré wrote down his account of the incident which he witnessed while serving as a sentry at a fort in the desert.

In 1912, a group of legionnaires were returning to base when they were suddenly attacked by a gang of Arab marauders. The soldiers were just two miles from safety when they were mercilessly cut down. Five of their group were killed before the attackers were driven away. The surviving soldiers dug makeshift graves and buried their comrades on the "battlefield". The searing heat and the danger of another attack made the option of bringing them back to the fort impossible. The burials had to happen there and then so that the bodies would not be pulled apart by animals. Stone piles marked the graves and the soldiers then marched back to their base.

Rene Dupré survived the attack and, two weeks later, he was on night duty guarding the fort. Aided by bright moonlight, Dupré saw a figure staggering through the desert. As the man got closer, Dupré was able to see that he was wearing the familiar uniform of the Foreign Legion. The sentry was astonished when he realised that he could see right through the mysterious figure.

The image was real and vivid, but Dupré knew that the harsh conditions of the desert could be playing tricks on him. He summoned his comrades to have a look so that they too could witness the ghostly apparition outside. Standing on the wall of the fort, the other legionnaires saw the transparent, staggering soldier. One of them recognised the ghost. It was Leduc, one of the men who had been killed in the attack. Once the group recognised him, the phantom disappeared.

A few nights later, Leduc returned and blood was seen dripping from his face; Leduc had been killed by a bullet in the head. Several nights later, a different spirit was seen and he was identified as Sergeant Schmidt. He too wandered in a zigzag fashion across the desert. The spirits of Leduc and Schmidt were the only two that the soldiers saw from the security of their barracks. Why those two men? they wondered. Why not some of the other soldiers who had perished in the battle? Leduc and Schmidt were very good friends, however, and the soldiers concluded that they were looking for each other.

The two spirits were never seen together until fifteen days after the first apparition had materialised. They were not frenzied, panicked wanderers this time. They appeared marching in step out of the desert. Before they disappeared over a sand dune, one of them lifted his arm and bade farewell to his living comrades. The ghosts were never seen again.

THE SHIPWRECKED WINNER OF A GRAND NATIONAL

Moifaa was a champion racehorse from New Zealand. Early this century, his owners decided to ship him to England and enter him in the prestigious Grand National Steeplechase. In 1904, the animal was on his way, making the long arduous journey by ship. Disaster struck and the ship was lost in a storm. Moifaa nearly drowned but managed to swim to a desert island where he roamed freely before being rescued.

He was sent on to England where he was duly entered in the Grand National. Competing against 25 other horses, he won by eight lengths.

THE AMITYVILLE HORROR HOAX

On 13 November 1974, Ronnie DeFeo butchered his father, mother, and four of his brothers and sisters. The address of the slaying was 112 Ocean Avenue, Amityville, New York. The property was a large Dutch colonial house with six bedrooms, a swimming-pool, study, a boathouse on the water and a large garden. The house was put on the market but, because of its grisly history, nobody wanted to buy it.

George Lutz, however, wasn't a superstitious man. He saw a fine property in good condition close to New York City and, best of all, a crazily low price tag of $80,000. George, his wife Kathleen, their three children Daniel, Christopher and Melissa, along with their dog, moved into their new home thirteen months after the DeFeo murders.

In January 1976 the Lutzes fled, never to return. They claimed that they were terrorised by a chain of ghosts and a series of bizarre events. Green slime oozed downstairs, hooded figures drifted through the house, windows crashed open and shut, sending dangerous shards of glass down on the children. Melissa spoke with a spirit pig named Jodie. A priest named Father Pecararo exorcised the house – all to no avail.

The priest was transferred to a distant parish; the Lutzes fled and a book called *The Amityville Horror* was written by a journalist named Jay Anson. This "true story" was a hit, a bestseller, and was turned into a blockbuster movie. Anson reported that the house on Ocean Avenue was built over an ancient well used by the Shinnecock Indians. This tribe used the site to hold their sick and insane before they died. They never used the site for burial, though, because they believed it was infested with demons.

As the royalty money rolled in for writer Anson and the Lutz family, the first sceptics emerged. The horrible weather conditions and phases of the moon described by the Lutzes did not match weather reports of the period. Historical records confirmed that the Shinnecock Indians never lived near the place. And, most alarming of all, the writer of *The Amityville Horror* never actually visited the house. He hurriedly wrote his book based on recorded phone interviews with the Lutz family.

Killer Ronnie DeFeo's lawyer, William Weber, boasted on local radio that the whole plot was concocted over a bottle of wine in Lutz's kitchen. The idea was his, he claimed. Weber went on to sue the Lutzes for his share of the book and movie profits. Judge Jack Weinstein did not believe the lawyer but did say "the evidence shows fairly clearly that the Lutzes, during this entire period, were considering and acting with the thought of having a book published."

After the Lutzes moved out of the Amityville house, the Cromarty family moved in. They experienced visitors and intruders of a different kind. They were so plagued with tourists and souvenir-seekers that they sued the Lutzes and the book publishers for invasion of privacy. They settled out of court. The author Jay Anson died in California in 1980 following heart surgery.

A TIMELY DEATH - ON FRIDAY THE 13TH

Austrian composer Arnold Schoenberg was born on 13 September 1874 and he believed that the number 13 would play a role in his death. As he entered his seventies, he noticed that, when he would hit 76, the sum of the digits 7 and 6 would total 13. He became convinced that something was going to happen to him at that age. He studied the calendar and, to his horror, found that 13 July 1951 fell on a Friday. On that fateful day, the 76-year old kept to his bed to avoid accidents. Shortly before midnight his wife checked on him, ready to tell him off now that the fateful day was nearly over. He uttered one word to her – "harmony" – and died at 11.47 pm.

The Austrian composer, obsessed with the number thirteen, died at 13 minutes to midnight, on Friday 13, aged 76.

FLIGHT 401

When Flight 401 crashed into the murky Everglades in 1972, all one hundred passengers and crew perished. Some of them lingered in agony as rescue workers hurried to the scene on that dark December night. Captain Bob Loft was trapped in his cockpit and lasted only an hour after the crash. He was dead by the time help reached him. Second Officer Dan Repo screamed painfully as he was pulled from the wreckage. He made it to hospital but died the following day.

What happened?

Studies of the black box recordings provided some clues. As Flight 401 approached Miami, signals in the cockpit showed that something was wrong with the landing-gear. It appears that, while the crew concentrated on solving the problem, they didn't notice that they were losing altitude. By the time they were alerted to the situation, it was too late. There was no time for a textbook crashlanding, no time for passengers and stewards to brace themselves. The plane struck the ground heavily – a lethal skid rather than a wreckage-twisting inferno.

At the crash scene rescuers found a chilling, almost unreal scene. The plane was like a wounded bird. There was no debris scattered for miles – but everybody died, all the same.

After the crash the plane's owners, Eastern Airlines, embarked on a morbid insensitive cost-cutting exercise. They scavenged parts from the ill-fated plane and used them in their other planes. Passengers innocently sipped drinks served from trolleys from a fallen aircraft. They had the use of fixtures and fittings after the previous users had been killed. Then the tale took an uncanny twist: ghosts appeared. Captain Loft, Deputy Officer Repo and some of the flight attendants were seen as shimmering shadows in planes carrying equipment from the tragic Flight 401.

These ghosts were witnessed on several planes, all of which had the common factor of using the scavenged parts. The sightings continued for over a year and news filtered through to the airline's management. Naturally, they viewed the stories with scepticism. Their reaction was to refer witnesses to the company psychiatrist. Many of the staff saw this as a first step to being fired and kept the stories among themselves.

Investigative journalist John C Fuller picked up the story and published a book called *The Ghost of Flight 401* in 1976. He found that a web of evidence had been systematically destroyed. Reports of passenger and crew sightings had been noted in the logs carried on all planes. Fuller found most of the crucial pages were missing. With the publicity generated by Fuller's book, and with more and more witnesses coming forward, Eastern Airlines finally removed all parts associated with Flight 401.

The ghosts of Repo and Loft were recognised by colleagues who had worked with them. Sometimes, staring at information screens in their cockpits, pilots and engineers would see reflections of people looking over their shoulder. When they turned around, nobody would be there. Once, a hostess reported a broken oven and a uniformed man repaired the circuit. Moments later the plane's engineer came to solve the problem. He was the only person on board capable of fixing the oven; the first repairman was a mystery. Based on the hostess's description, the ghost of Dan Repo had done the repair.

Captain Loft once made himself comfortable in a first-class seat. The flight attendant asked why his name was not on the passenger list. Loft failed to reply and the attendant sought help from her supervisor and captain. The captain recognised Loft and the ghost immediately disappeared.

The hauntings remain a mystery but the ghosts appeared to melt away once the airline company had the good sense and good taste to remove the old parts of Flight 401.

UNEXPLAINED UFO PHOTOS

Two clear photos of a UFO were taken in Oregon in May 1950. Paul Trent, a farmer, saw a disc-shaped object in the sky and ran for his camera. He managed to get two pictures, both of them taken in clear daylight. An untrained observer studying the photos could conclude that there was something small hanging from electricity lines, or there was something big in the distance. Experts at the time analysed one photo in detail and concluded that "it is one of the best UFO photographs analysed."

Was Paul Trent an elaborate faker and did the experts get it wrong? Years later the photos were subjected to the might of NASA technology. Using equipment that scientists developed for analysing satellite photos of earth, the NASA experts concluded that the Trent photos were genuine.

THE SIBERIAN EXPLOSION OF 1908

In 1997, the Hale-Bopp comet whizzed by, coming within 122 million miles of Planet Earth. In 1995, the Schumaker-Levy comet crashed into Jupiter. Was it a comet that crashed into Siberia in 1908, causing devastation equivalent to 1000 Hiroshima atomic bombs?

In June of that year, villagers in the remote settlement of Nizhne-Karelinsk watched a streak of blue light thundering across the sky. Seconds later there was a massive explosion, causing the ground to shake and knocking loose slates off houses. It was later discovered that the explosion occurred 200 miles from the village.

Meanwhile, a driver on the Trans-Siberian railway stopped his train. He had felt a shudder and was convinced that the train had hopped off its tracks. That was not the case. What the driver had felt was a shock wave from the explosion – which had just happened over 800 miles away.

Geologists all around the world registered the crash on their delicate instruments. People everywhere enjoyed spectacular sunsets created by swirling dust tossed into the upper atmosphere.

Curiously, no serious effort was made to investigate the incident. In the western world, nobody was sure of the source of the explosion. If they suspected Siberia, they would have to deal with a territory as vast as the near side of the moon. Ten years passed before a serious investigation began – and then the scientists were looking for something else.

Soviet scientist Lenoid Kulik was sent to investigate meteorite falls in Siberian territory. Doing preparatory work in Moscow libraries, Kulik came across scattered reports from local Siberian newspapers referring to an "incident" that had happened ten years previously.

With his curiosity ignited, Kulik continued his research. He read a report about a pillar of smoke shining more brightly than the sun; about reindeer herds that had stampeded and scattered; about farmers getting sunburned on one side of their faces and not the other. The scientist gathered all this evidence, but nearly another ten years passed before he convinced the authorities to let him get to the bottom of the mystery.

Siberia is a harsh, unforgiving land. Frozen rock-solid in winter, it is boggy, muddy and infested with mosquitoes in Summer. In March 1927, Kulik found himself getting closer to the point of impact. The devastation he encountered, almost twenty years after the event, convinced him that something terrible had happened. Not far from the banks of the Merkita river, Kulik observed a dead forest for as far as the eye could see. Trees everywhere had keeled over, flattened by a mysterious blast. All the dead trees pointed in the same direction, telling the scientist that he was still miles from the centre of the blast.

Imagine dropping a stone in a pond. Imagine the ripples spreading out in ever-increasing circles. Imagine flash-freezing that water, recording the pattern of ripples for generations. Something like that had happened in remote Siberia. Devastation spread out like ripples from the source of the blast. Years later, when Kulik first stumbled on the site, he knew he was only looking at a small portion of the pattern. The source of the "ripples" that had knocked the trees was still far, far beyond the horizon.

Kulik and his team trekked for several days. They crossed 37 miles from the rim of the devastation to its centre. All the fallen trees fanned away from this "cauldron", as Kulik named it. Strangely, some charred trees remained standing at the epicentre of the explosion.

They assumed that this was the place where a mighty meteorite had plummeted to Earth. On this and four subsequent expeditions, the Russian scientist found no metallic fragments of space rock. Kulik died convinced that the blast was caused by a falling meteorite.

The evidence, however, was confusing. The "cauldron" was the centre of the explosion but it was just a circular area, not a crater. Why were some trees still standing there? After 1945 a new theory emerged: the pattern of damage was similar to that caused by the atomic bombs at Hiroshima and Nagasaki – devastation fanning out from a centre; structures at the centre which partially survived. Old tales of blisters on reindeers and men now made sense. They had to be radiation burns, similar to the ones documented in Japan. The incidence of deformed animal offspring in the area was noted. By the time scientists moved in to the area with radiation-measuring equipment, fifty years had passed since the explosion. Radiation levels were normal.

The answer to the Siberian explosion can only be in one of three categories: it was man-made, set off by advanced alien life-forms or a natural event. A man-made solution is unlikely. The technology to unleash such power was not developed for nearly another forty years. The alien solution can't be proved or disproved. It will be believed by UFO buffs who want to believe it. That leaves the possibility of a natural phenomenon. What force could hit our planet, unleash such energy but still not leave a crater?

The comet theory is the most likely. When Halley's Comet whizzed by in 1986, scientists sent up the Giotto space probe. As the Schumaker-Levy Comet plummeted towards Jupiter in 1995, it was examined by the Hubble telescope and other sensitive equipment. The conclusion was that a comet is a ball of dirty ice with the density of soufflé. Scientists watched the muddy Schumaker-Levy ball of sludge hit Jupiter with devastating effect. The chances of a comet hitting earth are remote but very real.

In 1908 we all had a lucky escape. If that object, be it a comet or whatever, had hit our planet a few hours later some of the more populated areas of the world would have been in the line of fire. St Petersburg or London could have been hit. Luckily, the heavenly object made its impact on one of the few places on the planet where no human life would be lost.

JOYITA

The diesel-engined boat named *Joyita* was practically unsinkable. This twin-propellered ship had three separate holds all lined with five inches of cork. Captain Miller worked the Pacific with his little boat, hauling passengers and cargo between the islands. In October 1955, he and twenty-five passengers left Western Samoa to make the relatively short 270-mile journey to the Tokealu Islands. More than a month later, the ship was found abandoned and half full of seawater. The captain and his mate Chuck Simpson had disappeared.

Although the incident has been called the *Marie Celeste* of the Pacific, the *Joyita* was not in as good condition as her Atlantic counterpart. While the slabs of cork kept the craft afloat, one of the engines was not working and the radio equipment was faulty. There was no evidence of a quick getaway. The captain and his mate appear to have made rough-and-ready arrangements to make life bearable on their crippled boat. They had strung up a sail in such a way that it would provide shelter or catch any rainwater that might fall.

The basic problem was discovered in a dry dock in the Fuji Islands. Severe corrosion had eaten through pipes beneath a boiler and flooded the engine-room. A desperate attempt was made to stem the flow by stuffing mattresses into the hold. Two bilge pumps were unworkable because they had been poorly maintained and were stuffed with cotton fibres and other debris.

Captain Miller was used to the laid-back sleepy pace of the South Pacific. The *Joyita* used to be owned by a film director and it was commandeered for service during the Second World War. Miller chartered the ship in 1952 but he proved not to be much of a businessman. By neglecting his refrigeration equipment, he allowed several of his cargoes of fish to rot. It was not long before Miller ran out of money and couldn't afford essential repairs to his boat. He was a well-liked, honest man, if somewhat on the careless side. To keep him from becoming completely penniless, friends arranged for him to get a regular job ferrying people and cargo between Samoa and Tokealu.

Before he set out on that final voyage, Miller knew that his boat was in poor repair. He convinced the harbour-master that he could fix a faulty clutch while at sea. Nobody noticed the fault in the radio transmitter which would have limited the range of Miller's messages for help.

Somebody was injured in the boat, because investigators found blood-soaked bandages and medical equipment strewn around. Once the true extent of the emergency became known, the powerless passengers may have thought they were going to sink – regardless of any reassurance that Miller would have given about the cork-lined holds. Although the *Joyita* had no dinghy or lifeboats, all the floats strapped to her side were missing. Did the passengers jump overboard and cling to these, feeling they had a better chance than by remaining on board? Or was a new panic created by the arrival of pirates to the crippled ship?

The pirate ship theory is not as crazy as it sounds. A strongbox containing nine hundred and fifty pounds was missing. It was unlikely that anybody would take this heavy object with him if he was trying to stay afloat and alive. Life in the South Pacific was easy-going in the 1950s, and there were several unregistered small boats floating around. Maybe a gang of thugs took the money and forced the witnesses overboard. Why else would the passengers expose themselves to shark-infested waters?

It is unlikely that anything bizarre or paranormal happened to the people on board the *Joyita* but, like most unexplained nautical tales, the mystery remains buried beneath the sea.

The *Marie Celeste* was plagued by bad luck both before and after her mysterious experience in the Atlantic. She was originally called *The Amazon*, and seafaring lore states that it is unlucky to change a ship's name. The *Amazon* was built in Nova Scotia, Canada in 1861 and her first captain died two days after she was registered. She suffered slight damage on her maiden voyage and, during repairs, a fire broke out. The *Amazon* had at least four captains before she ran aground on Cape Breton Island. She was salvaged, sold a couple of times, and eventually ended up belonging to New York's Winchester shipping company. This wealthy company rebuilt the ship entirely and renamed her the *Mary Celeste*. Her ill-fated voyage across the Atlantic was under the American flag. After that, the ship was sold several times. Owners had difficulties signing up crews for the "unlucky" ship. A Captain Parker bought the ship and deliberately wrecked her in the Caribbean, hoping to claim insurance money. He was caught, but was acquitted on a technicality. He committed suicide two years later.

US NAVY DISASTER

On the evening of 17 December 1944, the United States Navy suffered one of its greatest Pacific losses during World War II. Aircraft carriers and destroyers were involved, along with supply ships delivering vital food, fuel and ammunition from the Philippines. Seven hundred and ninety officers and sailors were lost, either killed at their stations, falling overboard or going down with their ships. Three destroyers were lost and the aircraft carriers were badly damaged. Dozens of fighter planes were lost or wrecked beyond repair.

The enemy did not suffer a single casualty nor a penny's worth of damage. The destruction of Third Fleet Task Force 38 was caused, not by the Japanese, but by the weather. A savage tornado brewed, creating vast canyons within the sea. Ships were tossed helplessly amid towering walls of water and vicious winds; they slammed into each other, their 50,000 horsepower engines helpless in the onslaught of sledgehammer waves. The commander-in-chief of the Pacific Fleet, Admiral Chester Nimitz, described the ordeal as one of the greatest losses of the Pacific campaign.

ATTACK THE NAVY - SEND IN THE HORSES!

French cavalry under General Charles Pichegru defeated and captured a fleet of Dutch ships on 20 January 1795. Attacking Amsterdam, Pichegru found the Dutch fleet trapped and immobile in heavy ice. The general charged his horses across the solid ice and overwhelmed the ships and their crews.

HUMAN BODY CLOCK

Clark Gable was a Hollywood heart-throb and is best remembered for his role as Rhett Butler in *Gone With The Wind*. In 1960 he co-starred in *The Misfits* alongside the legendary Marilyn Monroe. The 59-year-old actor suffered a heart attack on November 6th and was admitted to hospital, where he seemed to be making a satisfactory recovery. American hospitals long have the reputation of being the finest in the world and Clark Gable could afford the the best that money could buy.

On the evening of 11 November, a retired Swiss importer, George Thommen, was interviewed on the *Long John Nebel Show*, a New York-based radio programme. Thommen's topic was biorhythms.

The basics of biorhythms are easy enough to grasp. The theory states that we are all governed by three basic cycles. Our physical cycle lasts 23 days, and governs strength, co-ordination, speed, resistance to disease and other bodily functions. Our emotional cycle, lasting 28 days, looks after our creativity, mental health and moods in general. The intellectual cycle lasts 33 days; it affects memory, alertness, and our ability to learn.

According to the theory, our three biorhythm "clocks" are set at zero on the day we are born. As we grow older, life gets complicated. We all admit to having our good days and our bad days. The biorhythm theory says that we will have a very bad day if our three cycles hit "low" on the same day.

Now, back to that radio show in New York. Everybody knew about Clark Gable's heart attack, and Thommen used the story to illustrate the biorhythm theory. He didn't work back and say that Gable had had his attack on a bad day. Thommen looked ahead and what he said was more ominous . . . On 16 November, he explained,

Gables's physical rhythm would be "critical". Thommen explained that the actor's condition would be unstable on that day. He would be in danger of a fatal relapse.

This news leaked out during the course of a popular radio talk show. It was entertainment. The public didn't take it seriously and no one warned Gable's doctors. On Wednesday, 16 November, the star had a second unexpected heart attack and died. Clark Gable's life might have been saved if essential life-saving equipment had been at his bedside. The doctor admitted as much later.

This was not a stargazer's prediction. Thommen was not a fortune-teller or soothsayer. He was an intelligent, practical man with a belief in the emerging science of biorhythms. His prediction was not clouded in ambiguous, woolly statements. He did not say "A tall, dark and handsome man will be stricken by bad luck next Wednesday". In fact, as an amateur scientist, he simply said that there was a high chance of a specific event happening – and he was right.

Take any of the three 23-, 28- or 33-day cycles. The theory says that, from zero, we rise to a "high" at the halfway point. Then we go downhill to the end of the cycle . . . and then things get better again. Because the three numbers are different, we usually feel a mixture of things – we are up physically, down emotionally, so-so intellectually.

Keep an open mind about biorhythms. They are taken very seriously in Switzerland and Japan. It has been reported that some Japanese pilots are literally grounded on days that their biorhythm charts give a bad read-out. The biorhythm theory is one that doesn't contradict science; it doesn't depend on star signs or tea leaves in the bottom of a cup. A good computer store might sell you a biorhythm programme and you can keep track of how you are. Amusement parks often have biorhythm machines: put in 50p, key in your date of birth and the machine produces a card with the information. Those machines usually have artwork showing a gypsy and a crystal ball. Pity.

> Your physical (23 days), emotional (28 days), and intellectual (33 days) biorhythms are all together at zero on only two days of your life: on the day you are born and on the day you are aged 58 years and 67 (or 68) days. The figure varies, depending on how many leap years you live through.

JAMES DEAN'S CAR

"Nothing in his life became him like the leaving it."

Shakespeare – *Macbeth*

When an actor named Nick Adams told James Dean to get rid of his brand-new Porsche sports car, the star brazenly replied that he was meant to die behind the wheel of a speeding car. Film stars Ursula Andress and Alec Guinness felt ill at ease with Dean's latest fast car. So did George Barras, a car designer who modified lots of Dean's earlier sports cars. James Dean made three films – *East of Eden*, *Giant* and *Rebel Without a Cause*, but he is best remembered for being killed when his Porsche Spyder crashed in September 1955. He was on his way to a motor racing circuit when the accident happened, about halfway between Los Angeles and San Francisco.

Hollywood was stunned by the accident and it wasn't long before strange occurrences began to become associated with the wreck of the car. Barras bought the wreck for parts and shipped it back to his garage. While being unloaded, the Porsche slipped and crushed the legs of a mechanic. There were also several accounts of minor accidents happening to people who popped in to have a look at the car in which James Dean died. One man gashed his arm off some jagged metal while attempting to pull on the steering wheel; another twisted his wrist while trying to wrench off a piece of bloodstained upholstery.

A wealthy Doctor McHenry bought the car's engine, and his colleague Doctor Eschrid bought the transmission. The two men indulged in their expensive motor racing passion and wanted to fit the high-quality parts to their own cars. On 2 October, 1956, both doctors had their first race in their own cars fitted with parts from the tragic Porsche. One doctor was killed, the other seriously injured. McHenry's car went out of control and struck a tree, killing him instantly. Eschrid's car turned over while he tried taking a bend.

Another enthusiast bought two undamaged tyres and took to the open road in his own convertible touring car. He was lucky: no injuries and only slight damage to his car. What happened? Both tyres had blown at the same time.

Barras, the owner of the car, was shaken by this list of events. His desire was to put the car into storage but the California Highway Patrol wanted to borrow the car and use it as part of a travelling road safety exhibit. Two such exhibits took place without incident, but just before its third outing a garage used by the police burst into flames. Everything except the Porsche Spyder was destroyed. James Dean's haunted sports car suffered just a few scorch marks.

The star was heading to Salinas, California when he was killed. A truck driver bringing the car to Salinas for one of the exhibitions was also killed. George Barkuis lost control of his truck but managed to jump free. The car fell off the back of the truck, crushing the hapless driver to death.

Two other accidents happened to trucks with the same haunted cargo strapped on board, but the last mysterious incident happened in 1960. En route from

Florida to California, the remains of Dean's car simply vanished. This was presumably the work of a souvenir hunter. This person had to keep his identity and the location of his haul secret. Perhaps the string of bad luck and accidents continues. Nobody knows.

A STRANGE EVENT IN THE SKY DURING WORLD WAR I

Far above the fields of France, six German planes were returning to their own lines after a dawn patrol. It was September 1916 and The Great War, as it was known, was raging furiously in Europe. Suddenly a British plane flew out of the clouds towards the German airmen. The enemy pilots probably thought that the solitary British craft was on a suicide mission, because it made no effort to dash away from their superior numbers. In fact, the Germans had to swerve out of the way in order to avoid a collision with the brazen British plane. Quickly, the Germans regrouped and attacked their easy target. They riddled the fragile biplane with bullets but, strangely, there was no response from the two British pilots on board.

The British craft continued flying in a wide arc, heading back to the safety of French lines. The German pilots suspected a trick, and feared they were being lured towards a more elaborate full-scale attack. One German pilot flew close to the mysterious British plane. The hairs on the back of his neck stood on end when he realised that the British crew were dead. They were strapped bolt upright in their seats staring blankly ahead. By some quirk, the two British aviators had been fatally wounded but all the critical parts of their machine were undamaged. The German pilot swooped in a gesture of homage and led his men back home.

Meanwhile, the British plane flew blindly back in the

direction of the French lines. Forty minutes later it ran out of fuel but, even then, a mysterious hand guided it safely to the ground. The plane, resting on the warm French air, glided smoothly to a flawless landing on an open field.

One bullet had killed both men but hundreds of other rounds had ripped up the plane – none of them passing through vital components.

BLUEPRINTS FROM A DEAD MONK

Legend has it that Glastonbury Abbey in Somerset, England was founded by St Patrick in the 5th century before he went to convert the Irish to Christianity. The legendary King Arthur might be buried at Glastonbury. In the Middle Ages, the abbey was a popular destination for pilgrims. The monastery grew in wealth and power and, over the centuries, new buildings were added. However, when Henry VIII broke with Rome and dissolved the English monasteries, Glastonbury was his prime target. He had it razed to the ground. The Church of England bought the site in 1907, but there were practically no traces of the original monastery layout. Their objective was to excavate the site but, having paid £36,000 for it, there were only meagre funds available to fund the archaeological work.

Architect Frederick Bond was given the task of excavating the site. If finances were not a problem, anybody could indulge in a pattern of hit-and-miss detective work: excavate a random spot; if something is found, keep digging; when you hit a blank, excavate more random locations.

Bond did not have the luxury of unlimited resources but his excavations proved to be a remarkable success. Within weeks Bond had touched various towers and walls. He even found fragments of stained glass windows and door frames. His success astonished colleagues and his reputation soared. He put his success down to a mixture of guesswork and luck, not daring to reveal his real secret.

After getting the job of excavating the old abbey, Bond approached his friend, John Bartlett, who was a psychic medium. During a seance in Bond's office, Bartlett made contact with a being who claimed to be a 16th-century monk named John Bryant. The soul of the dead monk took possession of Bartlett's body and proceeded to guide a pen across sheets of paper. The notes and sketches from this seance revealed plans and layouts of the old monastery.

Frederick Bond was startled. This written information seemed to be wrong; the layout of Glastonbury appeared different to what historians expected of an ancient monastery. However, Bond had to begin somewhere and he used the maps gathered during mystic seances.

Embarrassed about the unearned credit he was receiving, Bond wanted people to know the truth. After ten years of successful work at the Glastonbury site, Bond felt confident enough to let the world in on his secret. He published his story in a book called *The Gate Of Remembrance* – and instantly became a laughing-stock. His reputation was ruined. The Church of England paymasters cut his budget and assigned most of the work to more conventional operators.

Bond spent the next twenty years in America, a disillusioned and bitter man. He was, after all, the one who began the original excavations so successfully. No one would accept that his insights were channelled to him by a monk who had died nearly four centuries earlier.

HIGH COLUMNS SUPPORTING NOTHING BUT AIR

In 1689 English bureaucrats tried to tell Sir Christopher Wren how to do his job. The eminent architect had been commissioned to design the interior of Windsor Town Hall. The city fathers examined the work when it was completed and told Sir Christopher that there were not enough pillars holding up the ceiling. He would have to add more, they said.

He obliged and added four more pillars but the canny architect pulled a fast one. The extra pillars stop short of the ceiling. The authorities were fooled. The mock pillars, and Wren's building, are still standing today.

LIFE-SAVING DEATH SENTENCE

In 1902, Auguste Ciparis was a Negro who worked on the docks of St Pierre on the small Caribbean island of Martinique. He murdered a man, was captured, tried and sentenced to be hanged. He spent his days waiting in a small, thick stone-walled cell. A heavily-grated window let in some air and scant light. The door of this half-moon-shaped building was so small that the condemned prisoner had to crawl into his cell. There he lay, crouched, lonely, waiting to die.

All this time Mount Pelee volcano overlooking the town festered violently, belching ash and boiling water down on the town. The mountainside facing the town was glowing with red-hot lava and at breakfast-time on 7th May Mount Pelee exploded, hurling a wall of lava out of its way and sending a hurricane of flame down on the hapless town. Searing heat and flames killed 30,000 people that morning.

Ciparis had been waiting for his guards to bring him food. Suddenly he felt the prison crashing down around him and his body was badly burned by the intense heat.

Ash and fumes flew through his window and the prisoner feared a death worse than hanging. He was buried alive. "I smelled nothing but my body burning," he said afterwards. "Soon I heard nothing but my own unanswered cries for help." After three days, rescuers ventured into the town and found the prisoner in his cell, horribly burnt – but alive and sane.

He was reprieved with a suspended sentence. Ciparis spent the rest of his days earning his living as a sideshow with a circus. Complete with a replica of his cell, he was advertised as "The Prisoner of St Pierre".

DIVING FOR WATER, AND OTHER THINGS

"Cut a branch of Hazel on Midsummer Eve and it will serve as a divining rod to discover treasures and water. To procure this Mystic Wand, you must approach the Hazel by night on Midsummer's Eve, walking backwards, and when you reach the bush you must silently put your hands between your legs and cut a fork-shaped stick; that stick will be the divining rod and as such, will detect treasures buried in the ground. If you have any doubts as to the quality of the rod, you will only have to hold it in water – for in that case your true divining rod will squeak like a pig, but your spurious one will not." From a medieval German recipe.

In the Middle Ages, the fearsome Spanish Inquisition believed that the ability to find water by using a Y-shaped stick was the work of Satan. The Inquisition discouraged the practice and burnt repeat offenders.

Here's a story of a gifted water-diviner using his skills in a life-and-death situation: During World War I, British forces occupied the Gallipoli peninsula in Turkey. They were trying to control access to the Bosporus, which is a strait of water linking the Aegean Sea with the Black Sea, separating Istanbul from the rest of Turkey, and Europe from Asia. The Turks were confident that troops wouldn't be able to hold the peninsula because of the absence of water.

The resourceful British shipped in fresh water from their base in Malta, nearly eight hundred miles away. Of course, the Turks attacked these precious convoys and the British foothold in Gallipoli was, to say the least, precarious. Army engineers made attempts to sink wells, but to no avail. Then they heard about Sapper Kelly, an Australian soldier stationed with them.

He had a reputation for finding vital wells for cattle and sheep farmers back home. He wandered around with a Y-shaped strand of copper and, in no time, he had located water within one hundred yards of divisional headquarters. The engineers sank a well at the spot indicated by Kelly and soon they had a supply of 2000 gallons of water per hour. Before discovering Kelly, the engineers had sunk another well just fifty yards from Kelly's spot and had found nothing.

(For those interested, the Gallipoli campaign was a disaster, but it did not fail for lack of water.)

Michael Connolly, who is featured in the introduction, has had success divining for missing persons and lost property. He also claims he can use his divining rod to tell the difference between a pound coin belonging to him and a pound coin belonging to somebody else. He tells a story about a diviner in Lyons tracking a murderer. The event happened over three hundred years ago.

On 5 July, 1692 a man and his wife were murdered in a cellar in Lyons and the house was robbed. A diviner named Aymar set out to trace the criminals using his divining skills. He stood in the cellar where the crime happened, taking in the morbid atmosphere, getting a "feel" for the victims and their evil murderers. Walking from the cellar, he followed the unseen traces of the robbers to a shop he was certain they had visited. At all times he was accompanied by justice officials from the city. He stepped off the quays and into a barge on the River Rhone. His companions were baffled: how could this water-diviner follow the murderers' tracks while the watery signals from the river literally flooded his senses? Aymar persevered and traced the route of the criminals to another part of the city. Finally, Aymar's divining skills led him to a city prison. He assured his colleagues that one of the gang was already in their custody. His divining rod pointed at the prisoners and suddenly it twitched at a hunchback who had been arrested for petty theft.

This prisoner tried denying anything to do with the murders. Aymar confronted him with his account of where the gang had been since the crime and the hunchback broke down, stunned that this stranger knew so much about him. He confessed to his crime and gave the name of his accomplices.

Is divining the work of Satan or some other evil spirit? Hardly. How about Sister Martin, a nun who had the gift of being able to divine water. She was unable to suppress her talent even though her religious superiors discouraged her. Instead she developed a knack for finding relics; the holier the relic; the harder her hazel rod twitched.

Let us remember Arthur C Clarke's Mysteries of the First, Second and Third Kind. The gift of divining falls into the second category. How people find water and other things is baffling to us now but, in a few years, perhaps science will be able to shed some light on mysteries such as the ones highlighted in this *Pigs Do Fly!* collection.